THE
INCARNATE

KENNETH G. BEASON
&
JAMES L. CAVANAGH

THE INCARNATE

The Incarnate is a work of fiction. Though actual locations and real names mentioned in this novel may have representations in history, they are used in a fictional manner and the events and occurrences were invented in the mind and imagination of the author, except for the inclusion of such historical facts and historical characters that are interwoven in this novel. Without limiting the foregoing, all other names, characters, places and incidents either are the product of the author's imagination or are used fictitiously, and any resemblance to any actual persons, living or dead, events, or locales is entirely coincidental.

Published in the United States of America by Kenneth G. Beason.

Printed by Createspace.

ISBN-10: 0615925820
ISBN-13: 978-0615925820

To all those that venture into the imagination of writers and inspire us to tell our stories—our readers.

We would like to express our gratitude to the many people who saw us through this book. To all those who provided support, encouragement, offered comments, assisted in editing, proofreading, and design. Our deepest appreciation and admiration goes out to our friends and family for their patience, and encouragement.

A LETTER

To whom you may be,

As you begin to read these words in some distant future unknown to me, it is my hope that they will make sense to you. It is important that you heed these words I have written and hope that in some fragment of your mind there remains a trace of the memory that you, yourself—in another existence—asked me to do so.

It's most likely, if I still exist, we live separate lives, not knowing one another's name or where and how each of us live out our lives. It was in our last meeting that I was given a sense of the great, titanic struggle you have engaged in for so many years.

By the time you read this, you may have already gained some awareness of an innate knowledge about the darkness that works against you—that haunts you, and strives to destroy you by some horrible means. As incredible as that may seem, know that your feelings are not the ravings of someone who has lost their mind.

Just as in your previous life, it's likely that you have already suffered much in the present. It is my hope that your suffering will be eased by some of the answers you'll find in the following pages. It is more than a story. It is your history.

CHAPTER ONE

THE SOUND OF LABORED BREATHING cut into the quiet, steamy black of night. It grew louder and louder as a man moved hurriedly through the darkness. The urgency of fear relentlessly clutched at his throat, driving him. The beam of his flashlight jerked as he desperately rushed along, searching. He knew two things with certainty: what he was looking for was near and that he'd know what it was when he saw it. The light was falling on tombstones, monuments, and mausoleums with the frantic pace of his panting. Swinging wildly, the beam shined up into the moss-laden, ancient trees and then down to the ground at his feet. He stumbled, almost falling in his haste.

"Damn it!" He cursed himself in a hushed voice.

He moved forward again, searching. The light caught a white, stone mausoleum then strayed away. The man suddenly stopped; slowly, he brought the beam back to the structure. He started forward, his pace slowed to deliberate, cautious steps. Approaching directly towards the tomb's rusted iron door, he illuminated it with a now unwavering light. The man blinked his eyes against the sting from the sweat that rolled off his brow. Wiping his face, he dragged his hand down over his lean, haggard, middle-aged, features. His clothes were soaked and the breast of his shirt rose and fell with the heavy thud of his pounding heart. His eyes veered upward to see the name engraved into the white stone above the door. "Alexandria," it read. The man's mouth fell open, in shock.

"Oh God!" he said. "It's real. It's really here."

Reaching out towards the letters carved into the stone, he traced them with his fingers as though he needed to prove to himself what his eyes had already told him. Satisfied, he took a deep, shuddering breath and looked down at the iron door. Raising his hands warily, he pushed hard against it. Flakes of rust fell to the stone apron below, but the door didn't budge. The man's eyes narrowed in frantic concern for a moment before he cast the flashlight beam at the limestone blocks that surrounded the door. Above the name there was a cross shaped recess carved deep into the stone.

"Wha . . .?" he started, stopped, then stared in confusion for a moment. He moved off, walking around the crypt, using the beam of light to carefully examine its detail.

"Got to be something," he mumbled aloud, "I know . . . there's *got* to be a way!"

At the back wall of the vault, there was an iron cross inlaid into the stone. It was the same size and shape as the hole that was cut over the door. The man clawed at the edges of the cross with his fingernails, trying to pull it out. It wouldn't budge. Looking below the cross, he saw a decorative row of stones protruding across the width of the back wall. Instinctively, he pressed hard on one of the stones, it moved inward with a hushed creak. As it did, the iron cross moved out, extending inches from its stone encasement. His hand leapt up to the cross, grabbed it, and pulled. Wiggling it, he was able to pull it free. He held the piece of iron in his hand and examined it with the flashlight. It was an iron rod with identical crosses on both ends, resembling a spool. His eyes brightened and his hand suddenly closed tightly around the spool. He quickly made his way back to the iron door.

"Yes!" he said aloud. "It's gotta be!"

He placed one of the crosses into the carved out recess. It fit perfectly. Carefully sliding it in further, he could feel it seat itself into some metal mechanism. His hand tried to turn the cross, but it wouldn't give. Quickly, he laid the flashlight down on the stone apron at the foot of the door and placed both hands on the end of the key. His face contorted in effort as he strained to turn one way and then another. He let out a groan and, finally, the lock broke free. There was a metallic clank and the edge of the door came open an inch away from its frame.

The man took a step back, the thump of his heart now pounding in his ear. He bent to pick up the flashlight and pushed on the edge of the door. It slowly opened with a loud scraping sound. He was immediately hit by a strong, musty, acrid smell—a smell of great antiquity. Slowly, he brought the light up into the black of the interior. A misty haze drifted eerily through the air. There was no sarcophagus, no structure that could hold a body. Instead, it was packed with an array of ancient objects. Everything was covered in dust, but even his untrained eye caught the gleam of gold and the sparkle of gems. There was a stone bench that ran around the walls. On the bench and much of the open floor space, there was a display—almost a jumble—of flags, ornate swords, sculptures, and wooden crates. There was a shield with a golden, lion crest, and silver and copper vases. Searching, his light fell on a small, ironwood chest decorated with iron straps. His eyes narrowed on it. Stepping inside, he moved directly toward it.

He knelt down and pulled the lid of the chest open. It was filled with papers; handwritten loose pages, newspaper clippings, rolled up weathered scrolls, and ancient looking parchments. There were photos, old drawings, and etchings. An expression of fear and wonder came across the man's face.

"Lord," he said. "God please. Have mercy on my soul."

He laid his open hand on top of the contents, took a deep breath, and froze. Did he really want to know? He began sifting down through the papers. His fingers touched upon something. Taking hold, he pulled it out. It was a bronze, sun medallion with a broken, gold chain hanging from the top. His eyes examined it for a few seconds before he shoved it in his pants pocket. He stood, hurriedly searching with the flashlight. Finally, he stilled the light on a large, leather bag with a Coptic cross engraved on the front. Without hesitation he stepped to it, picked it up, and dumped the contents. As he shook the bag empty, a glittering cascade of gold and silver coins, and jeweled artifacts clattered to the floor. Heedless of the noise and the treasure, he turned back to the ironwood chest and began grabbing handfuls of the documents, quickly putting them into the bag.

Clutching the bag under his arm, the man hurried out into the night. He closed and relocked the door, and returned the key to where he'd found it. He knew in his bones that there was little time—he had to get back to Gainesville and find out what it all meant.

A half hour later, racing down the two-lane highway, his headlights cut into the hazy night. On the seat next to the man, lay the bulging, leather bag. In one hand, he held the medallion tightly. Staring ahead, his face knotted in concentration, his eyes watched the road while seemingly trying to unravel some inner mystery.

Ahead, he saw the flashing, hazard lights of a car stopped on the side of the road. He eased off the gas. Getting closer, he could see an older, gray-haired woman was trying to lift a spare tire out of the trunk of her car.

The man's jaw muscles clenched. "Can't stop now," he said aloud.

As he neared, the woman looked toward his oncoming car with a forlorn expression of helplessness. Without thinking, the man braked hard to a stop, reached across the front seat and rolled down the window.

"Need any help?" he asked. The woman only looked at him with uncertainty. He smiled at her reassuringly. "Where are you headed?"

"Palatka," the woman answered.

"Hang on," he said, "let's see if we can get you back on the road."

Cursing at himself under his breath for taking the time to stop, the man backed up and parked in behind the woman's car. Lit by his car's headlights, he worked swiftly to change the woman's tire. As he was finishing and putting the flat in the trunk, the headlights of an oncoming car came up the road and passed. His head below the trunk lid, wrestling with the tire, he did not see the car slowing down a short distance away. It turned into an old, farm road and came to a stop. Backing up onto the highway, the car turned around, and slowly headed back towards them.

"You've got about fifteen miles to Palatka," the man said, slamming the trunk closed. He came around the car toward the driver's side window where the woman was sitting.

"Make sure you get that spare replaced," he said smiling.

"Thank you so much," the woman said. "There's no telling how long I'd have been here if you hadn't stopped."

With the sudden roar of an engine, the man looked up. Holding his hand out, he tried to shade his eyes from the blinding headlights. The car was speeding toward them. Very close, at the last second, it veered straight at him. Before he could react, the car sideswiped the woman's car with a loud violent clash of metal, crushing the man between the two vehicles.

SAMUEL HOLDEN JERKED AWAKE as the pain of being crushed to death shot through his body. His youthful, handsome face, contorted in an agony beyond his years, was covered in sweat. He sat up quickly and, with trembling hands, pulled the sensor off of his finger. He grabbed at the electrodes that were stuck on his face and head, and ripped them away. Reaching inside of his sweat soaked pajamas, he yanked out the wire leads that were attached to his chest. He rolled his legs out to sit on the edge of the bed. His body quaking, his eyes lost in an inner agony, he wrapped his arms around his stomach and rocked back and forth.

"Hey! Hey! Hey! Calm down. It's okay, Sam, you're awake now. Everything is cool. Do you hear me?" Jessup Polk's voice came over the speaker mounted over the bed.

Still hugging himself, Samuel's eyes rolled up at the one-way glass window of the monitoring station. "Yeah . . . , I hear you," he said quietly, without conviction. He lowered his eyes and shook his head from side to side. It was always easy for them to say, he thought. Nobody understood what the dreams were like—that they could be so real. He took a deep breath.

"I'm coming in," Jessup said.

Samuel looked at the one-way glass window again, as though he could see Jessup watching him from the other side. In the four years he'd been at Meadowbrook the only meager comfort he'd had was knowing that Jessup was looking after him. He sometimes thought Jessup suffered almost as much as he did from just watching his night terrors.

The door to the monitoring station opened and Jessup's tall, heavy-set frame came into the sleep room. He was dressed in the green scrubs he always wore. With his size, his crew cut, and the tattoos that covered his arms, Samuel thought, he looked more like a bouncer than a grad student. But he knew the guy didn't have the mentality to hurt a fly.

Jessup's eyes looked at Samuel with a wary sympathy. Without a word, he walked to one of the chairs against the wall, sat, leaned forward, and with his elbows on his knees, held his head in his hands. "Sorry, Sam," he said very quietly. He said it as though he didn't want to intrude.

"Hey, man, I'm okay," Samuel said, managing to come up with a half smile. He hated to see Jessup suffering because of him.

"I know it was a bad one," Jessup said softly. His head was still down, looking at the floor. "The telemetry meters . . . all of them, heartbeat, respiratory, perspiration, and rapid eye movement . . . all of them off the charts."

"Dr. McGaffey will be thrilled," Samuel said. He knew that Jess had to interview him as soon as possible—McGaffey insisted on it. "You forgot the tape recorder."

Jessup looked up at him. "Screw McGaffey," he said. "Let's take it easy for a bit. You want coffee or something . . . juice?"

Samuel looked at him and shook his head. "No, no," he lied, "I'm okay, Jess. Let's get it over with. I don't want him getting on your ass again."

"Just give us a second," Jessup said, holding up a hand. "He's not gonna know when we recorded it. Just tell me, for now."

Samuel could tell he was trying to sound calm. Why did he waste his time trying to fool me? "What?" he answered.

"What happened this time, Sam? Did someone die again?"

Samuel nodded. "It was a man. He was hit—crushed—by a car." His dark eyes rolled up at Jessup. "I felt it, Jess," he said. There seemed to be a horrifyingly endless variety of the dreams, different people, different eras and places. The thing they had in common was that they always ended with someone's violent death.

Jessup frowned and his lips clinched.

Samuel knew that he was busting to say something. "Go ahead, Jess," he said, "spit it out."

Jessup rocked his head from side to side like he was looking for a place to start. "Look, Sam . . . ," he finally said, "I know you've pretty much decided about . . . what you're gonna do." He held up his hands to show he meant no harm. "That's cool, man, it's your decision."

"It's my life, Jess," Samuel said.

"I know. I know," Jessup added quickly. "It's just that with night terrors people don't normally remember them. They just sleep right through them. What I'm saying, Sam, is that there is something there that, well . . . , it scares me. I don't know that you'd be safe . . . if you . . ."

Samuel only looked at him.

"Hey, bud, I know, it's up to you," Jessup said. "I know you don't like meds, but maybe . . ."

Sam shook his head again. "No, thanks. Meds only makes the dreams last longer."

"You just have to keep telling yourself that," Jessup said.

Sam's eyes met Jessup's and took on a deep, penetrating, almost eerie focus.

Jessup flinched, blinked and looked down. "I mean that they're just dreams," he said. "You gotta focus on that, Sam."

The young man looked away. "No one will ever really understand," he thought. "There's something there. It was something a hell of a lot more than dreams." In his mind he could still see the bronze sun medallion. It was too real. He'd seen it again and again, so many times before. It had become a part of him.

CHAPTER TWO

TIMOTHY GODWIN SAT AT HIS DESK in the study of his modest home. The illumination from the blank, white page on his computer screen added years to his forty-five-year-old, still boyish face. He brought a medallion—a bronze, sun medallion—up to his face and stared at it for awhile before lowering his head and pressing it hard to his forehead. Lying the medallion down on the desk, he placed his hands on the keyboard and began to type.

Saint Augustine, Florida. The Fort Saint Mark: 1782

Breathing heavily, almost collapsing from exhaustion, Victor Wilton, a colonial settler on Florida's east coast, leaned heavily against the rough, outer stone wall of the fortress. His clothing was filthy and torn. Little was left of his shirt but strips of cloth, both pants legs were torn out at the knee. He looked up at the full moon that had risen out over the night blackened sea. There was an unsettling calmness in the air. The sea wind was only the barest breeze. The only sound beyond his weary breathing was the soft lapping of rippling waves washing onto the beach.

Victor's eyes were filled with fear. He ignored the physical pain of the bruises on his body and the blood that seeped from his swollen lips. He turned his head to look down the long, southern wall of the great fortress. He saw no one. Nervously licking his lip, he looked up at the round moon and thought of his wife and daughters—would he see them again? Suddenly, he jerked his head to his left, to the sound of steadily advancing footsteps.

The footfalls stopped, everything became quiet. Victor's eyes flicked about in terror. He was too tired to run. Then, a frightful, harsh scraping sound rent the night air, sending a chill up his spine, prickling his skin. To him, it was the unmistakable sound of hardened steel dragging against the stone wall—the hardened steel of a sword. It was close, just beyond the corner of the wall. Victor raised his sword, the scraping stopped, and a voice sounded from around the corner.

"How many times have I killed you over the centuries, Victor? Tortured you? Murdered your families?"

Hearing the cold, inhuman tones of Colonel Sebastian Loxton's voice brought a painful grimace to Victor's face. The voice, somehow known to his very soul, crawled through him with a chilling terror. The footfalls began again—Loxton was getting closer, and closer. Suddenly, there was silence.

Still out of sight, around the corner, Loxton was only a few feet away. Tall and stout, his battle-worn British officer's uniform was not in much better shape than Victor's shabby clothing. He held his sword up at the ready. "You realize you are the reason they have all suffered? Haven't you learned to leave me be? Or, is it your memory of them," he said, with something of a laugh creeping into his icy tone, "and their . . . shall we say . . . horrible and painful death . . . that drives you to seek me out?" Loxton could see Victor's shadow, his sword held high, on the stone foundation. A sneer came to Loxton's face. He spoke in a quiet voice, almost a hiss. "I suppose finding one's children lying dead, would leave a somewhat lasting . . . memory!" The last word was yelled as Loxton lurched forward and swung his sword around the corner of the wall. With a loud clank the sword hit nothing but the stone wall. Loxton looked in shock and surprise; his enemy had ducked, lowering to a crouch.

With a glaring hate in his eyes, Victor sprang to his feet. He moved so quickly that, in what looked like one movement, he pinned Loxton's sword hand to the wall, and thrust his own blade into his enemy's body. He brought his snarling face up, almost touching Loxton's. "My memories are all that I have," he said. "This is for my children." He pushed the sword in deeper. "And this is for those who were before them!" The snarl on Victor's face grew to an animal-like, vicious intensity; his eyes blazed in effort as he shoved the sword in deeper yet, up to the hilt.

Loxton's face went ash-white as his eyes lost their focus. Victor put a hand to his foe's chest and shoved, pulling his sword free. Loxton fell hard to his knees then collapsed to the ground. Looking down at the still corpse, Victor said, "I'll see you in the next life."

Instantly, a mist began to rise off Loxton's body. Smoldering, the mist quickly thickened into smoke. As it rose it began to spiral, forming itself into a ghostly shape, looming above the corpse. Victor's knowing eyes watched without alarm as the apparition of an ominous being began to take shape. Grinning sinisterly, its face became skull like, with beady, burning red eyes. It looked upon Victor for a brief moment before screeching loudly, then, suddenly, in a hissing flash, dissipated into nothing.

With no emotion on his face, Victor placed the point of his sword against his stomach, his hands, gripping the handle, were above his head. He closed his eyes tightly and, holding his breath, brought the sword down, thrusting it through himself. Slowly, he sagged against the stone wall and slid to his knees. He looked up at the moon and his eyes quickly lost the light of life.

CALVIN ATKINS WAS READING ALOUD from an open book, "At that moment, he was born again. Far from . . . ," he was interrupted by a woman's voice.

"Do you mind?" the woman asked.

With his expression blank and his mouth somewhat agape, Calvin turned around to look at the woman behind him in the line at the bookstore. She appeared to be in her mid-thirties.

"I haven't read it yet," the woman said, a hint of a smile at the corner of her mouth. She was pretty, with dark brown, shiny, shoulder-length hair and deep brown eyes. Her professional-looking gray suit enhanced her self-assured bearing.

Calvin was dumbstruck for a long moment and could only stare at her through the lenses of his large, outdated, black-framed glasses. His hand absently wiped away a clump of unruly brown hair from his forehead. Finally, he blinked in recognition. "Oh. Oh, yeah. My bad," he managed, his face reddening. "I wouldn't want to ruin it for you. I've already read it three times—but there's this one part . . ."

The woman glared at him and folded her arms across her chest.

"Right . . . , sorry," Calvin said. He gave her an embarrassed smile and turned back around just as the person in front of him stepped away. Sitting at a table with a stack of paperback novels was the author they were all waiting to see. A placard on the table read, "Timothy Godwin, author of *The Journeymen Diaries*." Calvin's mouth fell open again before he recovered and stepped forward offering his hand.

"Mr. Godwin, it's such an honor to meet you," Calvin gushed.

Timothy's eyes brightened and he smiled at Calvin's enthusiasm. "It's nice to meet you . . . ," he said shaking hands.

"Calvin. I'm Calvin Atkins, your biggest fan."

"Okay then, Calvin," Timothy said. He took Calvin's book, opened it, and began to write.

"It's so incredible how you come up with this stuff," Calvin said excitedly. "Victor and Sebastian battling each other over time. Killing each other off, only to be born over and over again into the next child that draws its first breath."

"Come on, man," came a male voice from the line, "give us a break."

Calvin looked back over his shoulder and grimaced apologetically.

Timothy smiled at him. "Don't give too much of it away, Calvin, you'll put me out of work."

"Yeah, right. Sorry," Calvin said, taking the book back. "You know I've got some great ideas. You could like—"

"No. No. No," Timothy said, holding his hand out at Calvin and smiling. "Thanks, but I've got it all covered."

"Oh. Yeah. Of course, I guess you have," Calvin said. "Thanks, Mr. Godwin."

"You're welcome, Calvin."

As Calvin stepped away from the table he risked a nervous smile at the woman behind him. She looked at him, clearly annoyed, and stepped up to the table. Calvin hurried away.

"Hello," Timothy said, taking the book from the woman and shaking her hand. "You are?"

"Tasha."

"Nice to meet you, Tasha."

"Do you get a lot of those?" she said motioning over her shoulder with her eyes at the departing Calvin.

"You mean Calvins?"

Tasha smiled at him.

"They're growing in numbers. Although I can't complain. Fans, like him, are good for business."

SAMUEL HAD HARDLY SAT DOWN in the chief psychologist's office before the bitterness and boredom began to seep in. He knew immediately where Dr. McGaffey was trying to go—right where he was always trying to go. He always said meaningless, empty words about having grown close to him and wanting to help him, but the wheels were always turning. Samuel looked into the doctor's eyes. McGaffey wore thick-lensed glasses that made his already large greedy eyes look enormous. He quickly perceived McGaffey's thinking about how desperately he wanted to do another paper about the dreams. The doctor looked down at the medical chart on his desk. Seeing the top of McGaffey's bald head, Samuel rolled his eyes away in disgust.

McGaffey looked up, his lips pressed together as though he were greatly concerned. "I don't know what to tell you, Sammy," he said. "Throughout the sleep study program, we've changed your diet, your medication, sleeping habits . . . your environment . . . counseling techniques, everything over the years." The doctor tossed his pen on the desk, leaned back in the chair, and held his hands out in frustration. "The only thing we've been able to ascertain—the only thing we know for sure—is that the nightmares are becoming more frequent, and more vivid and terrifying."

Samuel looked back at him. It wasn't even worth the small effort it took to read what McGaffey was thinking. "So, tell me something I don't know," he said.

The doctor pointed a finger at him and stood up. Heavy and short, he liked to pace behind his desk, taking little, wobbly steps. His face scrunched up in thought, he looked at Samuel, occasionally glancing down at the medical chart on the desk as he spoke. "Normally, through the same testing we've put you through, we have been able to isolate the root cause of most of our patient's nightmares—such as stress, phobias, trauma, insecurities . . . , psychosis." McGaffey shrugged and threw out his hands. "The list goes on. But, with you—we've not been able to find any associations." He stopped pacing and, with his hands on the back of his chair, leaned toward Samuel. "We haven't been able to find what's triggering your nightmares. And . . . there's the other thing. In describing your dreams, you can come up with detail about historical eras that no one your age and with your education could know. I've done research and talked to historians and anthropologists, Sammy. Experts on particular periods of time—they themselves were unable to match your knowledge of detail in ancient civilizations. They've expressed to me that your accounts ring true and have even given some of them new insight, new understandings."

"Yeah, that thing." Samuel said.

McGaffey pounded the desk weakly with his fat, little fist and his eyes glowed with hopeful pleading. "Do you have any idea what kind of ground breaking research that could lead us to? I could—we, Sammy—, *we* could be famous. Are you going to throw out an opportunity like this?" The doctor's eyebrows went up like he was sorry for Samuel. "I was just mapping out a groundbreaking, experimental program to—"

"And now," Samuel interrupted him, he had to swallow in distaste before he continued, "after four years, you've run out of time."

McGaffey blinked several times, averted his eyes, and then held up a hand indicating that he wanted to say more. He sputtered before he could get the first words out. "Well, I . . . that's not how I look at it, Sammy."

Samuel hated it when McGaffey called him "Sammy." He lowered his eyes and exhaled with impatience.

"We don't look at it as a time issue," McGaffey continued, "we look at it as a treatment issue. Here at Meadowbrook, we're only concerned about what is in the best interests of the patient."

"Yeah," Samuel thought, "and your best interest is in the research papers and grants you've gotten off of me." He looked back into the doctor's eyes, searching.

"Now, yes," the doctor said, "by law, if you insist on leaving—as of today, you're legally an adult—we have no authority to force you to stay." He gave a weak, embarrassed smile. "But, Sammy, I strongly caution you to consider the dangers. The nightmares devastate you here, in a controlled, therapeutic environment." McGaffey held a stubby, cautioning finger up. "Imagine—just imagine having the nightmares getting worse and worse when you're on your own with no support." He closed his eyes and shook his head at the horror of it. "You know, Sammy, your parents put you here because they loved you and wanted only what was best for you."

Yeah, his loving parents, Samuel thought. His eyes went inward and the bitterness flooded into his chest. His beautiful, mother, too consumed with her own beauty and too busy fooling around to care about anyone but herself. And she sure didn't have any use for a weak, feeble husband whose only objective in life was staying soused on scotch. From his earliest memories, neither of them ever paid him any attention except when something went wrong. Then, whatever was wrong, it was always his fault. Samuel shuddered, trying to shake the stinging memory of always knowing what they thought—what they *really* thought. It was hard on them because it magnified the guilt of being lousy parents to start with. Knowing that their child could somehow tell when they were lying and anticipate their actions terrified them. They didn't have the emotional capacity to deal with it. That's where McGaffey came in, offering them the easy out, even recommending, for "therapeutic reasons," of course, that they abandon contact with him. It was a perfect solution for everybody—everybody but him. He looked up at McGaffey, his eyes focusing into a penetrating stare.

"And," the doctor was saying, "I feel . . ." His voice fell off at the sharpness of Samuel's stare. "What do you see when you look at people like that?"

"Clarity," Samuel said. "Like, I can see that you know it is wrong to keep me here because you don't see me as a risk to myself or anyone else."

McGaffey blinked and sputtered again, "Oh . . . , no . . . well," he gave Samuel a sickly, sheepish grin, "it's much more complicated than that, Sammy. It's . . . it's what I don't see that worries me."

One side of Samuel's mouth curled up into a sardonic grin. "Don't worry, Doc. Because what you didn't see was that it was my parents that really needed to be here, not me." He stood up, and looked down at McGaffey. "It's time for me to leave," he said.

The doctor's face sunk in failure. "It is your choice, Sammy," he said sadly. "Wait." He opened a desk drawer, pulled out a plain, white, business envelope, and held it out to him. It had "Samuel" written on it. "They wanted you to have this if . . . if this day ever came."

Samuel recognized his mother's handwriting. He took the envelope, and ignoring the doctor's outstretched hand, turned to the door.

"Er, happy eighteenth birthday, Sammy," the doctor said, as the door closed.

Samuel made his way down the hallway, towards his room. His eyes narrowed against the familiar, soft, almost subliminal, elevator music, the dusty, plastic potted plants, and the brightly colored walls; all of it designed to mask the institutional stink of the place that, somehow, still screamed at him. After four agonizing years of being a guinea pig, he'd had all he could stand. In the day room, blaring from the TV, was the same game show that was on every morning at eleven. A small group of the residents sat close to the screen, some, their eyes pharmaceutically deadened, staring, a few others, curled up, dead asleep.

Samuel stopped. Jessup was sitting at a table in the far corner of the room. He was laying out cards from a deck, showing a new resident how to play solitaire. Jessup worked nights, he was never there in the daytime.

Spotting Samuel, Jessup stood up and walked toward him with a big grin on his face. "Well, Sam," he said, "today is the big day, happy birthday, man."

"Yeah," Samuel said, "the big day. What are you doing here, Jess? The night shift doesn't start until ten."

"Well—I got pulled."

"It was McGaffey," Samuel said. "Wasn't it?"

"Well, you know he and I never really saw eye to eye on things," Jessup said. "It's just his way of showing whose boss. I could just quit and leave, if I wanted to. They can't make me stay here. And, I guess, now, they can't make you stay here either, can they?"

They both grinned.

"Sam, I just wanna say . . . whatever you decide" Jessup's voice thickened, and he blinked and lowered his eyes.

"Aww, come on, Jess," Samuel said with a laugh. "Don't go all mushy on me. People might start thinking you really care about the residents."

Jessup grinned, reached into his pocket, pulled out a pen and handed it to Samuel.

"What's this?" Samuel asked.

"It's a pen," answered Jessup.

"I know it's a pen."

"Read it."

Samuel rotated the pen, it had the Institute's name, address, and phone number on it.

"Something to remember this place by," Jessup said. "I'm gonna be here for awhile. At least, until I get through my graduate courses. There's a whole new world for you out there and I know you'll do good. Be sure and send a postcard, when you get the chance." He smiled and pointed at Samuel.

Samuel smiled and nodded.

They shook hands and patted each other on the shoulder. Jessup said, "See ya', buddy," and started walking back into the day room. "Be sure you stay in touch, Sam. I'll be looking for that post card."

Samuel continued back towards his room. Passing the hallway to the sleep lab where he spent most of his nights, a jolt of fear and nausea swept over him. Feeling weakened, he put his head down and walked faster. He opened the door to his room and, with a dismissive grunt, tossed the envelope onto his tiny dresser. It didn't take but a few minutes to pack his small backpack. He wouldn't need much. Finishing, he looked around to make sure he hadn't forgotten anything. His eyes fell on the envelope.

Suddenly, Samuel felt almost frozen and slowly, almost like a mechanical man, lowered himself down on his bed. He covered his eyes with his pillow and lay still for several minutes, all the time literally feeling the presence of the envelope. Gradually, a raging anger built and tore at him; he didn't want to give his mother the satisfaction of saying her piece in a faded letter. At the same time, a part of him, a heavily scarred, stunted child, desperately needing love and affection, burned in bitter desperation to see what she'd written.

Finally, his eyes angry and glistening, he threw the pillow against the wall, jumped out of bed, and grabbed the envelope. It was sealed with yellowing, transparent tape. He ripped it open. Inside there was cash and a note. "Good luck with your life, Mother," was all it said.

"Thanks, mom," he said in a flat tone.

He counted the money, there were ten one-hundred-dollar bills. He stuffed them in the pocket of his jeans and crumpled the note and envelope. On his way out the door he tossed the wad of paper in the trash can. In a half-hour, after completing the discharge process, he walked out of the Meadowbrook's front door. Standing at the top of the steps, he tilted his head back, closed his eyes and savored the warmth of the sun on his face.

After a moment he bounced down the steps and started walking quickly down the long drive that led to the front gate. Still moving he looked back, his eyes burning into the face of the old building. He turned back to the drive with the steady, strong stride of a young man who had something to do.

CHAPTER THREE

TIMOTHY GODWIN SAT in the comfortable, stylish, leather chair on the set of channel seven's AM Gainesville. His leg bounced up and down nervously. On a backdrop behind him was a blowup of the cover of his paperback novel, *The Journeymen Diaries*; the image depicting a ghostly, old cemetery. He turned to avoid the glaring, studio lights and caught the eye of Dr. Nathan Kibbling. Timothy gave him a quick smile and averted his eyes.

Kibbling didn't seem nervous at all. Slender with sharp features and a perfectly groomed goatee, he looked very comfortable in a conservative suit and tie. He was every inch the self-assured college professor. His book, *Back from Before*, with an image depicting a tunnel of light, was displayed on the backdrop behind him.

"Five seconds, Miss Lester," someone from the crew called out.

The host, Miss Lester, a slim and pretty, young, black woman, hurried over and sat down between the two writers. She gave a dazzling smile at one then the other. "Ready, guys?"

"Two . . . one . . . ," the crew man said, then pointed at Miss Lester.

"Good morning, Gainesville. We have two special guests with us this morning, local writers who are making it big. They are Timothy Godwin, creator and writer of the best seller, *The Journeymen Diaries*. And Dr. Nathan Kibbling, for him, another best seller, *Back from Before.* It's a pleasure to have both of you here this morning."

Timothy managed an awkward smile for the camera. Dr. Kibbling only nodded calmly in recognition.

Miss Lester turned to Timothy. "In *The Journeymen Diaries*," she said, "your fictional character, Victor Wilton, lives through centuries of time by being reborn into one life after another. While witnessing events throughout the world's history, Victor struggles to find what will end his bond to the Earth. Originally, this book was published online and it became so popular it has now become a best-selling paperback." She looked at Timothy, her face screwed up in curiosity. "So, can you tell us how you came up with the concept of your story?"

Timothy hesitated. Beyond the host, Professor Kibbling was suddenly staring hard at him in rapt attention. "Well . . . , let's see," he began, "I've always had an interest in history. Often I would think about what it would be like to live in a different time period and witness, or be part of, actual events that took place." Timothy paused and took a deep nervous breath. "This is where Victor came to mind. He's basically a lost soul that doesn't know where he's lost from. He finds himself having to dig up his own past, through the use of his memories, in order to find out who he really is." Pausing again, his cheeks puffed with an exhaled breath, and his face finally seemed to relax. "He's become, in a wonderful way, a vehicle, if you will, to reveal details of history that most people don't know about—the good and the bad."

Miss Lester, nodding her head, smiled. "So, it's within Victor's memories that he begins his search?"

"Yes, yes that's right," Timothy answered.

The host turned in her seat to face Dr. Kibbling. "This brings us to you, Dr. Kibbling. In your book, *Back from Before*, you've investigated the concept of reincarnation."

The professor gave her a confident nod of his head.

"Being a theology professor," Miss Lester continued, "would you see this as a redirection in yourself?"

"No. Not at all," Kibbling said. "Reincarnation has been a belief in many religions and philosophies for centuries. What I've also found interesting, is that there are people that have no religious beliefs at all, but believe in reincarnation. Many of them feel that they themselves have had past lives. And, surprisingly, some of them know things they couldn't know otherwise."

"That's amazing," Miss Lester said.

"Oh, yes, there are many, verified examples." The professor removed his stylish, black framed glasses and looked at Miss Lester like he might have been addressing an eighteen-year-old student in one of his classes. "Documented accounts of this begin to create questions of whether or not something—like Timothy's fictional concept of *The Journeymen Diaries*—may be closer to the truth than people realize." He looked at Timothy and the focus of his eyes sharpened into an intimidating stare.

Standing just in front of the set, the director held up five fingers and began counting off. Miss Lester thanked the guests and broke for commercial. A stage hand helped them remove their microphones and directed them to the wings.

"How do you feel?" Nathan asked Timothy.

Timothy responded with a relieved smile. "I'm still a little bit shaky with these things."

"I was too at first," Kibbling said, allowing himself a casual smile, "but you'll get used to it—and you need to. I'm confident this won't be your last show."

Gilbert Louden, a well dressed, short, fat, balding man approached and shook hands with Kibbling and Timothy. "Great show guys," he said smiling. "Shows like this really boost sales."

He looked at Timothy. "I can't thank Nathan enough for bringing your book to my attention."

"Well," Kibbling said, "I could see he was going to need a good agent and since I had the best . . ."

The men laughed.

"I've set up more interviews and signings, Timothy, and," Gilbert said, waving a playful finger in the author's face, "are we finishing up that second volume?"

"I'm working on it," Timothy said, swallowing.

"Make it good. I don't want people to think that you're a one-hit wonder. Ya' got a good thing going here, let's keep it happening."

"Yes." Timothy said. "I'll keep you posted."

Gilbert's cell phone set off a jarring, punk rock ringtone. "See what I mean," he said looking at the phone. "Sorry guys, I gotta take this." He pointed at both men. "I'll call you later." He walked away answering the phone.

"Does he ever slow down," Timothy asked.

"You better hope he doesn't," Kibbling replied. "We should get together and celebrate. Would your family be interested in getting together this evening?"

"Oh, thanks, but the wife and kids are out of town, my sister-in-law's baby is due and they're lending a hand with her other kids."

"Well, it's always exciting to have a new life brought into the world—all the more reason we should celebrate, even if it's just the two of us."

"I guess we should," Timothy said. "I'd love to."

SAMUEL KNOCKED, THEN WAITED at the door of a rundown, duplex apartment. Finally a sleepy Calvin Atkins opened the door.

Calvin stared at the young man, his mouth agape and wiped a scraggly clump of hair form his face before it hit him.

"Sam?" Calvin said. "What? . . . Man, you're all grown up."

Samuel smiled at him. He was surprised how good it felt to see Calvin again after his years away. "How you doin', Calvin?" he asked.

"Sam! I can't believe it! Hey, come on in."

The two shook hands and half hugged, clapping each other on the back, and went inside.

Samuel looked around the room. There was nothing fancy, just the basics. A jumble of DVD's, magazines, and books covered the coffee table and, on top of that, was an open pizza box with the contents half eaten. The only thing that looked neat were the collection of action figures that were displayed on shelves that ran around the walls just below the ceiling. A bookcase against the far wall was stuffed with books, mostly paperbacks, comic books, and papers. Beyond an old sofa and a couple of mismatched, stuffed chairs, there wasn't much else. Samuel smiled. "This is Calvin alright," he thought. For the first time he could remember, he had the feeling that he was home.

"I never thought I'd see you again," Calvin said excitedly, "after you and your folks, well . . . , moved away. How did you know where to find me?"

Samuel gave Calvin an "aw come on" look.

"Mom," Calvin said.

"Yep," Samuel said smiling. He motioned toward the bookcase. "I see you're still into books."

"Yeah, yeah. I even work at a Tremont book store, so I can get discounts . . . in fact, I met Timothy Godwin."

"Who?"

"Timothy Godwin, *The Journeymen Diaries*?"

Samuel shook his head.

"It's about these two guys that keep killing . . ." Calvin suddenly stopped and his eyes narrowed. "You still have those nightmares, don't you?"

Samuel shrugged his shoulders.

"Come on, Sam," Calvin said, ushering him toward the center of the room, "sit down. Are you hungry, man?" He grabbed the pizza box and they went into the kitchen and heated the leftovers in the microwave.

Later, eating in the living room they each gave a quick review of their lives since their last meeting. Samuel tried to brush by the years at Meadowbrook.

"I can't believe . . . ," Calvin said, chewing pizza at the same time, "your folks put you in an institution. Are they still fighting?"

"I don't know for sure, they were the last I remember." Samuel said with embarrassment. "I don't think they know any other way."

Calvin, leaned forward on his elbows, stopped chewing, and looked up at Samuel with his mouth open. "You telling me you haven't seen your folks in all those years?"

Samuel cocked is head to the side, shrugged with his eyebrows, and gave Calvin a grimacing smile.

"Wow, so much for the parent of the year award. I'm sorry, dude. So, what are your plans? What are ya' gonna do?"

Samuel could see the concern and pity Calvin was feeling. "It's okay. I'm pretty much on my own, after four years in that place I'm just fine with that. I've got enough money to get started."

Calvin jumped up, his eyes filled with excitement. "Hey, I could use a roommate—to split the rent. Oh . . . , and, hey, I could call and see if there might be an opening at the book store. If you're interested."

Samuel smiled. "Yeah, I'm interested." He gave Calvin a serious look. "You know where I've been, Calvin. And . . . I know—back when we were in school—people talked about me, being a bit strange and then going away and all. If you want to wait a while to think about—"

"What? There's nothing to think about, Sam," Calvin said, interrupting him. He laid a hand on his friend's shoulder and grimaced. "Anyone that ever talked about you, didn't know you. They were just being stupid. You had a bunch of crap to deal with your whole life that they didn't know about. And, I never told anyone. You're moving in with me. Where's your stuff?"

Samuel smiled, holding up the backpack. "You're looking at it."

"Well, that makes things easy," Calvin said. "Oh, the job. I'd better let Liz know before she hires some goofy freshman instead of you." He turned his head, squinting and looking around the room, then bent and started searching through the debris on the coffee table. "Where the heck is my—" He glanced up. Samuel was holding his cell phone. "How'd you find it? Samuel handed him the phone and just smiled. Calvin started to dial. "Hey, can you still do that trick?" He moved one hand behind his back, extended three fingers and waited with the phone to his ear.

"Three," Samuel said immediately.

"Are you ever gonna tell me how you do that?"

Samuel held up his hands, wiggled his fingers, and widened his eyes. "Magic," he said smiling.

CHAPTER FOUR

TIMOTHY GODWIN MADE HIS WAY up the walkway of the very large, split-level home. With a bottle of wine under his arm, he swiveled his head back and forth, his eyes wide in wonder. "Wow," he said under his breath. He rang the doorbell and waited, rocking back and forth nervously on the balls of his feet. As the door opened, his mouth fell open. A stunning, young woman, who couldn't have been more than eighteen, was smiling at him. She had a childlike face with captivating, blue eyes, her long, loosely curled, blond hair draped over her shoulders.

"Uhh—hi," he managed.

The girl gave him a dazzling smile. "Hello, Mr. Godwin," she said.

Timothy smiled back at her and put a hand to his chest. "Oh, have we met?"

"I saw you on TV with my dad. I'm Rebecca," she said offering her hand.

"Oh, of course," Timothy said. He awkwardly pulled the bottle of wine from underneath his arm and reached out with his free hand and took hers. "I'm Timothy."

"Honey, let the man in," a woman's voice called from the inside.

Rebecca smiled and stepped aside, "Please, come in."

He handed Rebecca the bottle. In passing, his eyes fell to her waist, the small round swell of an early mid-term pregnancy, obvious on her lithe body.

A mature, beautiful, tall blonde, standing just beyond the foyer, greeted him. "You'll have to excuse, Rebecca. You're the first celebrity she's met." The woman said extending a hand. "I'm Patricia, Nathan's wife. We're so happy you could come by."

"Well, it's a pleasure to meet both of you, but I assure you I'm no celebrity."

Nathan came up behind his wife. "You shouldn't be so modest," he said, approaching and wagging a finger, "people will take advantage of that if you're not careful."

Timothy smiled and shook hands with his host. "Well, at least I have you to show me the ropes."

Nathan put an arm around Timothy's shoulder and led him into the house. "That could very well be the best decision you've made in your life."

Timothy's nervousness quickly melted away in the pleasant, light conversation at the dinner table. By the end of the meal they had grown close enough to be comfortable in casual conversation. When they had finished eating, Timothy stood up and announced that he insisted on helping with the clean up.

"I wouldn't allow it," Patricia said.

Nathan waved his hand, signaling Timothy to join him. "While I hate to drag you away from your, beautiful and adoring fans," he said indicating Patricia and Rebecca with his eyes, "I think you and I have business to discuss." They all laughed as he ushered his guest down a hallway and into a large library like room.

"Wow," Timothy said, looking around the imposing room. The oak paneled walls were lined with shelves of books, many of them obviously very old. Spaces between the shelves were filled with paintings in ornate, heavy, gold frames. Along the tops of the shelves were ancient looking vases, some of silver, marble busts, and several armored helmets. "You must be a collector, Nathan, I'm very impressed."

"If you're alive enough years you seem to accumulate things. Please, sit. Shall we have a drink?" he asked.

At one end of the room was a large, ornate desk. In front of it, several chairs, upholstered in brown leather, formed something of a private alcove. "Of course, thanks," Timothy said. He walked across the room, and sank into one of the chairs.

Nathan walked over to a corner and opened an oak paneled door to reveal a small bar. "Scotch? An excellent choice for the successful author, sets just the right mood. On the rocks?"

"That'd be great."

The two men drank and talked about the ins and outs of writing and marketing books. While Nathan was at the bar refreshing their drinks, Timothy leaned back in the chair and looked at the room again in the relaxing perspective of the scotch. "This room is perfect. You've done well for yourself. Did Gilbert make all this possible?" Timothy asked.

"Hardly," Nathan answered, clunking ice into glasses, "Gilbert's a good agent and publicist, but it has been personal investments that have made all this possible."

"Well, you'll have to let me know who your broker is. I could definitely live like this."

"That's very possible, Timothy, now that you've joined the ranks of those having written a best seller.

"It wouldn't have been possible without you setting me up with Gilbert."

"Give yourself some credit. I know your father would have been very proud of what you've accomplished."

The smile fell from Timothy's face, and he lowered his eyes. It took him a moment to answer. "Thank you, Nathan," he managed.

"I want you to know that your father was a good man," Nathan said, handing him the glass.

"I . . . uh, thanks. I didn't know you knew him."

"It was only for a short time," Nathan said. "Because of him, I was able to see more clearly about some things . . . that . . . troubled me. My life took on a whole new direction, after seeing him. It was enough that I attended his funeral. I was quite amazed by the number of people that were there." He paused, giving Timothy a sympathetic smile. "I'm not sure that you realize the number of lives he touched. Perhaps it was fate that you and I have met. It has given me the opportunity to help you, as he helped me." Nathan looked down at his drink. "It's too bad that people often don't meet one another until some tragedy brings them together."

Timothy gave a somber, appreciative nod in agreement.

"Helping to get your work published was the least I could do out of respect for him." Nathan raised his eyebrows. "Oh, that reminds me!" He stepped over behind the desk, opened a drawer, pulled out a hard covered copy of *The Journeymen Diaries* and held it up in triumph. "This is the very first, hardcover print, I asked Gilbert to get it for me." He handed the book to Timothy. "With my complements on your sterling achievement."

Timothy stood and took the book. "I don't know what to say."

"There's no need to say anything, but, I must admit," Nathan said, looking at his guest with a teasing smile. "I'm very curious to see where you take this in the sequel."

Timothy turned his head to a movement at the door. Rebecca was standing in the open doorway. Nathan stood and walked over to her.

"I just wanted to say good night," she said smiling, "and that it was nice to meet you, Mr. Godwin."

Timothy smiled. "It's been very nice meeting you too, Rebecca."

"Goodnight, Daddy," she said as her father neared.

Timothy watched the young woman lift her face to kiss Nathan. Her father placed a finger under her chin and gently kissed her fully on the lips. Timothy' lifted his brow in surprise and quickly looked away. Rebecca smiled politely at Nathan, turned and left the room.

After she'd left, Timothy said, "It's got to be hard for you."

"What would that be?"

"Well, your daughter . . . , she's so young, to have to grow up so fast."

Nathan shrugged. "Yes. But, she's the least of my worries."

"What about the father?" Timothy said. He looked up to see Nathan's brow knit and his jaw muscles tighten.

"If it's all the same, Timothy, I'd rather not discuss this any further."

Timothy's face reddened. "I apologize," he said quickly, "I didn't mean to be intrusive."

"Apologizing isn't necessary. I appreciate your concern, but there are some matters that I don't discuss openly."

"No, of course, I understand," Timothy said. Both men were silent for a few long moments before he added, "Well, it is getting late. I should be going. I have a lot of work to do if I'm ever going to finish the new book." He placed his glass on the bar.

"Yes," Nathan said, "I insist you get on with it. I do look forward to reading it." He walked his guest out to the driveway where the two men shook hands and said goodnight. There was something of a quizzical look on Nathan's face, as he watched Timothy's taillights disappear around the corner at the end of the street. He was suddenly startled by a large presence, very close, and moving toward him. To his left, a young man, tall, and athletic with broad shoulders, was approaching.

"Excuse me, sir," the young man said. His voice was surprisingly deep for his age.

Nathan stilled and swallowed hard before managing a reply. "Yes . . . hello," he said.

It was obvious the young man couldn't have been far out of high school. He had neatly trimmed, red hair. His features were handsome and sharp with the confidence of someone who wasn't afraid to express himself in the adult world. "Hi, I'm Nick Stratton," he said, offering his hand.

Nathan ignored Nick outstretched hand. "What is it I can do for you, *Nick*?" he asked.

"Rebecca Kibbling lives here, right?" Nick asked. He withdrew his hand and patted his thighs awkwardly.

Nathan's posture stiffened and his face flushed with indignation. He spoke now with an icy, measured clarity. "And who, exactly, are you—, Nick Stratton?"

"A friend of hers. We went to school and graduated together . . . I was just wondering how she was doing."

"I would think if you're a friend of hers you would know how she is doing, wouldn't you?" Nathan said coldly.

"Well, after the graduation party, I went out of the country for awhile and we kind of lost touch. I don't mean to intrude, but I haven't been able to reach her, so, I wanted to come by and see her."

"That may be, but can you tell me why I would stand here, at this hour, discussing my daughter's private affairs with a complete stranger?"

Nick's eyes went round in surprise. "Wow," he said, "you're her father?"

Nathan stiffened with anger. "Excuse me, if that surprises you," he said stepping closer to Nick.

"I didn't mean anything, sir, and I apologize for coming by so late, it's just that . . ."

"Just what? I'm somewhat older than you'd expect? I believe this conversation is over."

Nick held up his open hands. "Oh—no, sir. I don't mean to be rude, Mr. Kibbling. Look," he said, starting to speak quickly, rushing to get his words out, "I'm concerned about Rebecca, I've been leaving messages, but I haven't heard from her. I just wanted to find out how she's doing," He hesitated a second then continued, his voice almost breaking. "I just don't understand. I know Rebecca, she'd be seeing me if—"

"If what? If she knew you were here? Look—Nick—do you and I both a favor, go find yourself another girl, before you find yourself in far more trouble than you can deal with. Again, this conversation is over. Now, get the hell away from my house and do not come back."

Nick looked stunned. "Mr. Kibbling," he said, his voice struggling with frustration, "please, again, I apologize for coming by like this. The last thing I want is to cause any problems for Rebecca or her family. Good night, sir." He turned and started walking away. At the end of the driveway he stopped and turned around. "Please understand," he said, "one way or another, I have to see Rebecca again."

"You have no idea of the trouble you're looking at. I would leave right this moment if I were you."

Nick shook his head in frustration and walked away. Nathan watched him walk across the street, get into a small car, and drive away.

TIMOTHY DROVE ACROSS TOWN to his home and went straight to his study. Waiting for his computer to boot up, he opened a desk drawer and pulled out a large, worn, canvas bound journal. Handling it with care and reverence, he opened it and turned through pages of small, neat hand written script until he found his place. He set his hands on the keyboard and, with his eyes on the log, began to type.

Germany: 1945

Bright, morning sunlight flooded through the windows of the General's Hall in the North Tower of Wewelsburg castle. The windows were set evenly around the circular room, twelve windows set back in twelve columned, arched alcoves.

Escorted by two, uniformed, armed Nazi SS officers, Fuhrer Adolf Hitler strode into the large, formal room. The loud, hurried thud of their boots on the marble floor echoed against the round, high-domed ceiling. The faces of the men were taut and showed no heed as they stomped across the large, dark green, sun emblem that was inlaid into the floor. Two uniformed, SS sentries guarding a door, came to attention and snapped out a straight armed salute as the men approached. One of them opened and held the door while the men passed through without any acknowledgment.

Inside the room, Reichsfuhrer-SS Heinrich Himmler was conferring with another uniformed SS officer. Himmler was middle-aged, slender, and wore glasses with round lenses. There was nothing physically impressive about the general. In civilian clothes he could easily pass as a bank clerk, but everything about the man's bearing, his posture, the cold, detached eyes, and the uplifted chin, spoke to his comfortable sense of authority. A second, younger officer, Obergruppenfuhrer-SS Henrik, tall and handsome with almost yellow blond hair and blue eyes, listened intently to his superior.

Standing beside his desk, Himmler said, "You must be absolutely certain everything is ready—" On Hitler's entry, he paused and only glanced up at the German leader. The young Henrik snapped to attention and shot out a Nazi salute while Himmler pointedly looked away and continued what he'd been saying. "They must be ready on my order, do you understand?"

Hitler raised his hand briefly, signaling Henrik to stand at ease, and glared at Himmler, his mouth narrowing.

The languid gaze of Himmler's eyes showed no sign of recognition of the fuhrer's distress. Calmly, he spoke to the junior officer. "Henrik, you are dismissed. See that the preparations we discussed are made."

Henrik nodded, saluted and turned to leave.

The fuhrer looked to his body guards, raised his hand and gestured toward the door. "Leave us," he said tersely.

Hitler and Himmler were left alone in the room. The fuhrer waited a moment after the door closed. The dark face of the man contorted in rage and his lower lip quivered. His eyes bore into his subordinate, his voice was barely able to contain his full anger.

"I am still the Fuhrer, Herr Himmler!" Hitler all but screamed.

No reaction was visible on the SS leader's face beyond something of an amused sneer tickling at a corner of his mouth. Himmler stepped forward and, without warning, slapped Hitler hard across the face. "You have lost this war, Fuhrer," he said with contempt.

Hitler's eyes went round, stunned by the force of the blow and the outrageousness of the affront, then the rage crept back in his face. He reached into the pocket of his trousers and, fumbling in his hurried anger, pulled out a small, Walther automatic pistol. Hitler leveled the gun only inches away from his target, directly between Himmler's eyes.

"How dare you!" Hitler hissed, the pistol quivering with his rage.

Himmler did not flinch. "How dare you fail the Fleischgeworden!" he said.

A cloud of doubt crossed the dark anger of the fuhrer's face. Very slowly, as though on its own, the Walther lowered. "The Fleischgeworden?" Hitler asked, a tinge of fear washing into the edges of his voice. "He is here? Who is he?"

Himmler allowed himself the barest flash of an evil grin then spoke coldly. "The American, 3rd Armored Division, is advancing. They are currently south of Paderborn. You can die here, Fuhrer, or run back to your hole in Berlin." After the briefest moment his cold, apathetic stare cowered Hitler and the leader looked away.

"Then go," Himmler said with contempt.

Hitler's eyes glazed over, slowly he put the pistol back in his pocket, turned, and with his head bent, started to walk toward the door. He placed his hand on the door lever and hesitated for an instant, before he opened it and left.

BURNING TORCHES MOUNTED on dark, heavy, stone walls cast an eerie, unsteady light over the ritual chamber, that was hidden in the depths of the castle. Red, double-sided banners with a white circle and the Nazi black swastika at their centers were hung from the ceiling. Below the banners stood twelve men, anhangers—ominous, evil appearing figures in SS, black, ritual uniforms of medieval armor. They faced one another in two ranks, their heads bearing dark skeletal faced helmets. The anhanger's formation flanked the foot of two spiraling, iron staircases. The steps led upward on either side, to the top edge of a circular, iron vault. A black, Nazi sun symbol emblazoned the face of the vault. Above the opening at the top of the vault, four great chains suspended its heavy, flat, circular, cast iron lid. From a platform, behind the vault, a hazy smoke and a sulfuric stench emanated from a large iron ladle. The glow of the white-orange, molten steel that filled the ladle dully illuminated the iron smelter behind it.

At floor level, a dark and menacing figure suddenly entered from an arched portal. Also dressed in a black hooded cloak, he wore a silver, skeletal mask. Around his neck a medallion hung from a silver chain, it was a black sun medallion with an SS symbol in the center. At a respectful distance, he was followed by the tall, blond, Obergruppenfuhrer-SS Henrik. As the masked figure passed between the ranks of the anhangers each lowered their heads. Without showing any notice of his attendants, the man ascended the stairs. There was a sense of inevitability to the steady, unhurried cadence of the thud of his heavy jackboots on the iron steps. At the top of the stairs, without hesitation, he descended into the vault with Henrik following.

The anhangers sprang into action. Immediately there was a loud clang, then the creaking, metallic sound of the great chains straining as the lid began to lower into place. With a dull, hollow clunk the lid seated itself on the rim. One of the anhangers, pulled down on a chain that steadily tipped the iron ladle forward. Its hot glowing contents poured slowly, sizzling into a channel that ran around the rim of the vault, the molten metal rapidly circled the seated lid. The white-orange quickly began to turn red, cooling and hardening, sealing the vault air tight.

Inside the vault, at the bottom of the stairs, the man in the silver, skeletal mask came to a stop and looked out at the small, self contained, well lit operating room that lay before him.

On the operating table, covered by a sheet, was a young woman with blond hair and Nordic features. Her midsection bulged with late term pregnancy. She was conscious but her eyes revealed nothing beyond a catatonic stare. A male doctor and a female nurse, dressed in operating whites, were standing by the table. There was tension in their eyes as they looked to the black cloaked figure. Henrik stepped back to the wall and waited in silence.

The doctor swallowed and moved forward, closer to the masked man. "Mein Herr—Fleischgeworden," he said nervously, "she isn't ready yet. It's too early."

The Fleischgeworden looked up. The doctor followed his gaze to the edges of the closed lid of the chamber. It glowed red hot from the heat of the sealing iron. Turning, he looked down at the pregnant woman, and walked over to her. The doctor obediently scurried after him. With a black, leather gloved hand the Fleischgeworden reached out, yanked the sheet from the woman, and let it fall to the floor, exposing her. "Cut her," he said without emotion.

Beads of sweat dotted the doctor's forehead, a look of doubt came to his eyes, but he immediately went to work. Placing the tip of a scalpel on the woman's belly, he cut carefully. A line of bright red followed the path of the scalpel. In seconds, blood streamed down over the pale, white skin of the woman's belly.

The Fleischgeworden casually watched the doctor work while his hand reached inside of his cloak and emerged with a dagger. Its shiny, pointed blade gleamed in the glare of the operating lights. The end of the handle was ornately crafted into a symbol: the SS black sun. He placed the point of the dagger against his cloak, at his chest. At the first sign of the baby's head, with both hands, he thrust the dagger, up to the hilt, into his heart. He stood immobile for a long second, staggered forward a step, and collapsed to the floor.

Obergruppenfuhrer Henrik knelt down and reached underneath the skeletal mask to feel for a pulse. He nodded to the doctor. Henrik stood up and nervously watched as a faint, misty vapor rose from the body's remains and evaporated into nothing.

In that same moment the doctor pulled the infant from the now lifeless body of its mother. The baby gasped, drew its first breath, and began to cry. The nurse took the newborn, quickly washed it, dried it, and swaddled it in a blanket. Finished, she handed the baby to the doctor. With a tense smile, the doctor cautiously walked over to Henrik and held the newborn in front of him. The Obergruppenfuhrer nodded and motioned the doctor to the stairs.

Outside of the vault, the anhangers reacted to the steady thud of pounding on the sealed cast iron lid. One of them lifted a black, leather gloved hand in signal; two others began working a two-handled winch. The heavy chains clanked and squeaked in sudden strain. The machinery groaned in effort for a few seconds before, with a loud bang, the lid snapped its seal. Large pieces of the hardened, iron seal flew free, they clattered down the metal stairs and against the stone wall and floors. The heavy lid swayed as it was hoisted higher.

The anhangers were silent, their rapt attention on the top of the now open vault. The doctor emerged from the opening carrying the swaddled infant. At the top of the stairs he stopped, his solemn eyes slowly scanned the ghastly lit chamber, settling on each of the anhangers in turn. Finally, he raised the newly born child above his head in triumph, as though an offering. Almost as one, the anhangers fell to one knee and lowered their heads in reverence.

CHAPTER FIVE

A DELIVERY MAN CAME THROUGH THE FRONT DOOR of the Tremont bookstore in downtown Gainesville. He was pushing a hand-truck stacked with boxes. The man looked impatiently at the employees working behind the counter.

Calvin walked over to him. "I'll get that," he said, smiling. He signed the delivery receipt, craned his head to look around the store, then called to his boss. "Liz, do you know where Sam is?" he asked as he leaned over to one side, trying to see past the displays in the center aisle.

Liz, a smartly dressed middle-aged woman, was waiting on an older woman at the cash register. She gave Calvin an annoyed glance over the top of her glasses. "Thank you," she said, smiling at the customer, "have a nice day."

Calvin was still looking at her. "Liz—"

"The last I saw him was over in history," she said, interrupting him.

Samuel was gliding a finger across the spines of the books in the world history section. In the week he'd been working at the store, he spent his breaks and any down time he had looking through the history books. He had a fascination—some deep sense of connection—to the bits and pieces he'd been able to uncover.

His finger stopped on *The War in Europe*. He pulled the book out, opened it and flipped through the pages. There were black and white photos of bombed and burning cities, starving children, Nazi soldiers, and stacks of naked, emaciated corpses. The images burned into Samuel's mind. Transfixed, his eyes lost focus. "What was it?" he asked himself. "I know I've seen this before." It was something—something like the inkling memory of a dream, but more vivid, almost something tangible that he could reach out and touch.

LIEUTENANT ROBERT KEMUEL of the 83rd Armored Reconnaissance Battalion, hurried across the square at the center of the devastated, abandoned village. Making his way through the chaos of assembling troops and tanks, he moved toward what was left of a small church. The clattering of the tank engines and the listless calls of the bone-weary troops dogged his ears. At a makeshift table set up amongst the rubble near the alter, the general commanding the 3rd Armored Division and Captain Steven Darnell, Kemuel's company commander, were looking at a map. The general was pointing at it and making sweeps with his finger while saying something to Darnell. Kemuel waited by the door for a few minutes until, finally, the captain saluted the general and came toward him.

"Where we going?" Kemuel asked Darnell.

The captain walked past the lieutenant and out the door. His eyes, hardened by months of combat, were washed in the tired, sadness of war. "Wewelsburg," he said over his shoulder.

Kemuel stopped and Darnell looked back at him. "Are you coming? We leave at first light," the captain drawled in his Southern accent.

The lieutenant started again, hurrying to catch up. "Do you think we'll get him?" Walking in stride with Darnell he pulled out a pack of cigarettes, he knocked one out, put it in his mouth, and lit it.

"Sergeant Collins," the captain yelled across the village square at his first sergeant, "make sure all the water cans are full—all of them." He turned to Kemuel, "Himmler?"

"Yeah, Himmler."

"I don't know, Robert," Darnell said, his eyes squinting far off into the glow from a bursting, artillery shell. "There's no doubt that he knows we're coming. When we get there, we're to secure the grounds. Not one soul is to get out of Wewelsburg, until they're cleared."

"I hope we catch the son of a bitch." The lieutenant let out a stream of cigarette smoke, looked around and lowered his voice. "If you ask me, he doesn't deserve a trial."

Darnell glanced at his junior officer and said, "Don't worry. If we do catch him, and he's who I think he is—there won't be any trial."

The captain's tone stopped Kemuel in his tracks, he stood frozen with the cigarette halfway to his mouth. "What the hell does that mean, who do you think he is, that we don't know already?" He watched as Darnell walked away without responding.

"SAM, PLANET EARTH TO SAM," Calvin said, looking at Samuel who was staring into the World War II book with a dazed look on his face.

Samuel realized his name was being called. He blinked away the powerful images in his mind and slowly turned his wide eyes to Calvin's concerned expression.

"We got another shipment to put up, man," Calvin said. "It's been busy up front and Liz's kind of in a mood." A look of worry came to his eyes. He stopped, and leaned down closer to his friend. "Hey, pal, are you okay?"

Samuel could see that Calvin was worried. The last thing he wanted was to be a problem for him. "Yeah, I'm good. Where's it at?" he asked.

"Got it up front."

Samuel followed Calvin out of the isle and toward the front of the store.

ALEX WEBB LOOKED UP to see Timothy Godwin standing in the doorway of his office in the research department of the museum. "Timothy," he said, smiling broadly under his brushy mustache. "Back to do more research on the new book, I presume." Alex was short and wiry, his hair was thinning, and he always seemed to be in a good mood.

Timothy smiled at him. "I can't believe you're actually glad to see me after all the work I've put you through. I feel guilty, it's like I'm abusing you."

"Nonsense, I live and breathe this stuff," Alex said. "I'd probably do it for nothing if the university quit paying me. But, hey," he paused and put a finger to his lips, "don't spread that around. They might take me up on it."

The men laughed.

"Besides," Alex continued, "I really like your work. What have we got today? Oh, by the way, I still have your other stuff in the back." He stood, walked to the door and headed down the hallway. Timothy followed behind. "Saw you on TV. You're getting pretty popular."

Timothy gave him an embarrassed smile. "Well, it could be short lived if I don't get this second book finished."

Alex led him into a research room in the back. There were shelves filled with reference books, displays containing an assortment of ancient, handmade tools, bones, pottery, crafts, and scraps of apparel. Along a back wall, Alex looked at the numbers on the line of grey, built-in, safe-like cabinets. "Thirty—eight," he mumbled to himself. Squatting, he began twirling the combination lock dial on secure unit number thirty-eight. He had the door open in a few seconds and turned around with a bulging, overstuffed, leather briefcase. "Here, ya' go," he said, lying it on a long work table.

Timothy looked at him hopefully.

Alex shook his head. "I'm sorry, Tim, I have no idea what language or form of hieroglyphics those were written in. They seem to go back farther than anything I've ever studied."

Timothy blinked away his disappointment. "Well, I appreciate your trying."

Alex shrugged. "I don't even know of anyone you could take them to."

Timothy nodded. "I think there might be someone else, but I wanted to give you the first crack at it."

Alex groomed his mustache with his thumb and finger. "One thing I do know, the manuscripts are priceless. I think you really need to get them into a safe and secure archive."

Timothy nodded, reached into his pocket and pulled out the bronze, sun medallion. "Can you tell me anything about this?" he asked, handing it to Alex.

Alex sat down at the table and examined it closely before he spoke. "Another piece of your collection?"

"Yeah."

"I'd love to know where you get this stuff," Alex said with a coy side glance.

"A writer never tells his secrets," Timothy said with a forced chuckle.

"Well, I had to try," Alex said. He leaned back in the chair and looked up. "It looks like a ziersheible, to me. An ornamental disc—a kind of metal jewelry used during the European Iron Age, to pin a tunica or belt pouch."

"So, you're telling me it's a button?"

Alex grinned then looked back at the medallion, his eyes narrowing in curiosity. "Then again . . . you know . . . this does look a lot like . . ."

"What?"

"One second," Alex said. He got up and hurried out the door and returned shortly with a large, old book. Sitting down at the table, he put his head down and flipped rapidly through the pages. "Here," he said, holding a finger on an illustration depicting a circle within a circle with twelve jagged bands connecting the two. "You're gonna love this. Look, it's called a black sun, an occult symbol used in Nazi mysticism. And here—," he said, flipping the page. His finger pointed at another image. "Here we have . . . the Wewelsburg sun wheel, a mosaic in the center of the floor of the Obergruppenfuhrer-hall—that would be the General's Hall—in the north tower of the Wewelsburg Castle, in Germany." Alex looked up at Timothy, "That's the very spot that Heinrich Himmler marked to become the center of the world—and it would have been . . . if Hitler had won the war."

"Himmler." Timothy said, blinking in recognition of the name.

"Yeah, Heinrich Luitpold Himmler, Reichsfuhrer, head of the Schutzstaffel—the SS." Alex slid the open book over in front of Timothy and tapped Himmler's picture. "Hitler carried the gun, but it was old Heinrich that squeezed the trigger, killing millions of innocent people through death squads and concentration camps. Extermination camps really, that's all they were."

Intrigued, Timothy stared at the picture. "So, what all happened at Wewelsburg?"

"Himmler set up a concentration camp there for his own slave labor but as far as what took place in the bowels of Wewelsburg Castle, no one really knows."

"Why is that?" Timothy asked.

"Because, Himmler ordered it to be destroyed . . . so it wouldn't fall into the hands of the allies. As to what happened to Himmler, questions remain, for many historians."

Timothy looked at the medallion and then at Alex, his eyes narrowed in curiosity. "Why's that," he asked.

The curator pulled back from the table, placed his hands behind his head, and looked up at Timothy. "History tells us that Himmler was caught by the British Army, but it is rumored that the man they caught wasn't Himmler—," Alex paused, clearly enjoying himself, "but a double."

"So, what happened to the man they caught?" Timothy asked.

"He committed suicide by crushing a vial of cyanide potassium in his mouth."

Timothy stared at him in confusion. "So, wha . . ."

"And, one other thing you might find interesting—it's been said Himmler believed he was the reincarnation of King Heinrich the first." Alex looked at Timothy questioningly. "It surprises me that you wouldn't know that, considering the basis of your first book."

Timothy looked away staring off into space.

REBECCA KIBBLING'S EYES GLOWED and a smile of contentment tugged at the corners of her mouth as she looked through the colorful infant clothing on the store rack. She was in the boy's section of "Baby Bubble," an upscale infant clothing store in the Oaks Mall. In spite of having promised her mother she wouldn't "go crazy" and buy anything before her shower, she took a baby blue, cotton sleeper off the rack, held it against her nose, inhaled deeply, smiled, and carried it to the checkout counter.

The heavyset, middle-aged lady at the register smiled at her. "Oh," she said, "a boy, that's wonderful." She took the sleeper from Rebecca and held it up. "That is the cutest little outfit, I wanted to buy it myself and, honey, I haven't had a baby in twenty years." They both laughed. "Is that all you needed today?"

"Yes," Rebecca said. "And, I don't really need that, but . . ."

"Oh, I know, believe me." The woman found the tag on the sleeper and ran a handheld scanner over it. "Your first?"

"Rebecca's cheeks reddened. "Yes, yes it is," she said.

"Well, sweetheart, it's a wonderful time. You don't worry about anything but taking care of yourself and enjoying it."

"Thank you so much," Rebecca gushed as she took the bag from the clerk. She left the store and headed for the mall exit.

Nick Stratton was sitting alone in the bombardment of noise in the mall's crowded food court. He disinterestedly picked at a small plastic tray of nachos. His handsome, bright features were uncharacteristically slack with boredom. His eyes stared off into space, focusing on nothing while a river of shoppers passed before him. Suddenly, his eyes sharpened, catching a glimpse of a long, loosely curled, blond haired girl moving on the far side of a knot of slower walking, shoppers. Nick half stood and bent to his right, trying to get a better look.

"I can't be that lucky," he said under his breath. He jumped up, ignoring the scraping of his chair and hurried after her. Quickly making his way through the crowd, he was tall enough to be able to see and follow the brief sightings of bouncing, blond hair. The girl was headed for the exit. By the time she reached the exit and placed her hand on the door, he was close, no more than fifty feet behind her.

"Rebecca?" he called through the din of diners and shoppers.

At the sound of his voice, Rebecca's body jerked, her shoulders came up, and she hesitated for a mere second before hurrying on out through the doors and into the parking lot.

Nick broke into a jog. "Rebecca!" he called again as the door closed. A group of four elderly women came in and lingered at the door, forcing him to slow to make his way through. "Excuse me. Pardon," he said nudging by them. Finally, he was able to burst out into the bright sunshine. Cars were cruising slowly by looking for a space close to the entrance. Nick stopped. His eyes scanned the crowded lot looking for Rebecca's blond hair. He caught sight of her two lanes over. She was pulling out her keys as she approached her blue Nissan. Without looking, he broke into a full run causing a car to slam on its brakes.

"Rebecca!" he yelled loudly.

Opening her car door, Rebecca tossed her bag in the back seat and was hurrying to get in the driver's seat.

Nick grabbed the open door before she could sit. "Rebecca," he said, heaving to catch his breath. "Where . . . have you . . . been? I've been going nuts. Didn't you get . . . my messages?" Her eyes were wide, almost panic stricken as she seemed to struggle for words. "What's wrong?" he asked, his voice softening with concern.

Speechless, she was only able to shake her head.

Nick looked down and stared for a second at the bulge of her belly. Slowly, his eyes, twisted in confusion, came up to her face.

"I need to go, Nick, please," she said, her voice cracking. She turned to get into the car.

"Wait," he said, gently touching her arm.

Rebecca's frightened eyes scanned the parking lot quickly then looked at him. "Please," she said.

"Look, I thought we had something special," Nick said, "and now . . . you're having a baby?" He stared at her. "What happened?" he demanded.

She spoke very quickly. "You don't have to concern yourself about the baby. There's no need to." Moving her head slightly to look past his shoulder, her eyes suddenly narrowed in fear and her jaw began to tremble.

Nick turned around to see what she was looking at. A man, tall, with light blond hair and dark sunglasses stood two rows away implacably staring at him. He was dressed in a long-sleeved, white shirt, a black tie, and black slacks. The clothing didn't hide his obviously lean, muscular body. Nick turned back to Rebecca. "Who's he supposed to be?" Her eyes flashed to her left. Another man, with same clothing, hair, and physique was glaring at them from further down the row.

"I have to go, Nick," Rebecca said, getting into the car. She started the car and pulled on the door, forcing Nick to let go. The door slammed shut. She started the car and began to quickly back out of the parking spot.

Nick stepped back to avoid the car's sudden movement. "For cryin' out loud, Rebecca. Let me help you!" he yelled.

As Rebecca braked to shift into drive, she rolled the window down a crack. "Just go, Nick," she said, tears rolling down her cheeks. "Forget about the baby and forget about us. Just stay away. Please. Our time is over." The car lurched forward and she sped away.

"Damn it!" Nick said. He turned toward one of the men in the dark sunglasses. With determination in his eyes, he began walking directly at the man. The man, still watching impassively, showed no reaction. Just as Nick closed on his target, a large, black sedan pulled to a stop and the man got in. Nick stopped and watched the car go to the end of the parking lot then turn and come back down four lanes away, where it stopped and picked up the second man. Standing on his toes, he was able to see the car stop at the mall exit and turn left, going in the same direction that Rebecca had gone. He watched it disappear in traffic. "What have you done, Rebecca?" he said aloud.

CHAPTER SIX

FOR THE REST OF HIS WORKDAY and through that evening, Samuel couldn't get his thoughts and feelings about World War II out of his mind. Waves of great emotion swept over him at odd moments, a feeling of sadness tinged with dashes of horror that made him tremble. It seemed to be teasing him, calling to him, telling him that there was something there that he had to know. He didn't say anything to Calvin. Hoping to get it out of his mind, he went to bed early and found himself tossing and turning for most of the night. It wasn't until the last hour of darkness before morning that he fell into a deep sleep and began to dream. The stark reality of the images flashed through his mind like a damaged film jumping its track.

CAPTAIN DARNELL SLOGGED THROUGH THE MUD leading his company forward. Coming over a rise he and his lieutenant could see the horizon, the smoke filled sky glowed a dingy orange.

"What the hell could that be?" Lieutenant Kemuel asked.

"Wewelsburg castle," the captain said, his voice soured by frustration, "and it's burning." He turned to the company strung out single-file behind him in the dark. "Step it up, men!" he yelled, "we're running out of time."

Darnell's mind was focused on one thing: getting there— getting *him*. For a while there was no sense of time, only an immeasurable period of muddy, black darkness—punctuated by the chaotic, shattering flash and boom of artillery. The scene was grim with fear and horror, and, at the same time, lasting both an instant and forever.

The captain found himself standing within the ruins of the burned out castle, his eyes intensely transfixed on a charred, but still intact door. Throwing and pushing smoldering debris out of his way he moved directly to it. He stared at the door, his eyes burning in determination, he reared back and drove his boot into it with the full force of his weight. The frame splintered with a loud crack. He shoved it open. The beam of his flashlight cut through the darkness, revealing a narrow, spiraling, staircase leading down into darkness. He took a step inside. Suddenly, there was brief flash—an image—a woman's face. Her skin was milky white and lifeless, her wide open, pale-blue, dead eyes stared directly at him.

SAMUEL BOLTED UP OUT OF HIS NIGHTMARE, gasping. He grabbed frantically at his chest, looking for the electrodes, but there were none. Disoriented, he looked around and realized he was home, in his room at Calvin's. Wiping the sweat from his brow, he tried to recall the dream, but there were only bits and pieces. It was as if his mind was blocking out something it wasn't willing or wanting to reveal. Breathing heavily, he lay back down and stared at the ceiling, trying to focus. What was beyond the door? He told himself he had to remember the dream, closed his eyes and drifted back to sleep.

LIEUTENANT KEMUEL WAS BEING ESCORTED through the old German psychiatric hospital by two enlisted army orderlies. The heavy thud of their boot heels on the stone floor echoed down the dingy hallway. From behind the locked steel doors lining the hall, the voices of madness drifted through the ancient building. Men mumbled nonsensical phrases, someone repeated loud grunts over and over again, some whimpered and cried like children, rounding it out was the random punctuation of a loud, terrifying shriek.

"Jesus," Kemuel said, as they walked, "this is worse than the goddamn front. How long have you men been here?"

"Too long, sir," one of them, a short, talkative soldier with a New York accent said. "Since the army took it over at the end of the war. Eight fun filled weeks. Not only with our boys, but the ones that were left here when the krauts left. Every one of them gone out of their minds. Doubt any of them will ever make it back home, unless it's in a wooden box." He stopped and held up a hand. "This is it, thirty-four." Turning to the door, he slid open a steel plate covering a small peephole and looked into the cell. Straightening up, he pulled a large, brass key from his belt. "This guy is one of the quiet ones," he said. "They scare me the most."

"Why's that corporal?" the lieutenant asked, his voice edgy.

"They're like snakes. They look you in the eyes as if they know you're afraid of them. Then all at once—they strike. They don't give no warning." He unlocked the door, opened it, and held it open.

Kemuel stepped inside. A man, in a straight jacket was balled up in the far corner of the tiny, dank room.

The head of the man slowly lifted. His weary, red eyes were sunken into the gaunt, ashen face. He looked at the visitor and squinted against the light of the doorway before a glint of recognition came to his eyes.

"Captain?" Kemuel said, his voice unable to hide his shock. It was Captain Steven Darnell. In spite of himself, Kemuel flinched at the sight.

A smile came to the captain's face. "Hello, Lieutenant," his parched voice said. "It's good to see you."

Kemuel blinked nervously and diverted his eyes. "You too," he said.

The captain looked down and chuckled, then looked up at the escorts. "Would you two thugs mind if I had a private word with my lieutenant?"

"Sorry sir, we're under strict orders—," the orderly started.

"Let me talk to him alone," Kemuel said. "What the hell can he do, bite me?"

The orderly hesitated a moment then shrugged. "Like I said, Lieutenant, we're under strict orders, sir." He looked Kemuel hard in the eye.

"Leave us alone, damn it! That's an order," demanded the Lieutenant.

The orderlies stepped out of the room, closing the door behind them. Kemuel walked slowly over to Darnell and knelt down in front him.

"I tell you what . . . ," Darnell said and swallowed.

"What's that, Steve?"

"The noises in this place can drive a man insane."

After a second of silence they both laughed. Then Darnell's eye's narrowed in seriousness. "I was hoping you'd come see me."

"I had to. What the hell happened to you in Wewelsburg? All at once, you suddenly lost it. Why?"

Darnell blinked his eyes several times, seeming to be looking for an answer. "I can't tell you," he finally said. "It's better that you don't know."

"I can't help get you out of here if you don't tell me."

"If you really want to help me, Robert," the captain said, his eyes searching Kemuel's face, "see that I'm buried back home."

Kemuel shook his head. "Like hell I will. You're not gonna die here, Cap. We're going back together."

"Just listen to me. Make sure all my personal effects, the ones you signed for when I was brought here, are buried with me."

"Don't talk like that, Steve," Kemuel said, "it'll just keep you here longer. We've all got battle fatigue—"

Darnell shook his head. "No, they can't keep me here." An urgency came into his voice. "Just promise me you'll do as I ask."

Kemuel stood, walked to the door and knocked twice. He looked back at Darnell and gave him a supportive smile. The door opened.

The captain looked at him intently, his eyes imploring. "Okay?" he asked.

Kemuel nodded as orderly swung the door open. "If it comes to that," he said, "you've got my word, Steve, but I intend to see you stateside."

Darnell watched the door close and waited for the sound of the lock latching into the frame. Alone in the semi-darkness, his eyes seemed to go inward into some other plane of existence. "It's time for a new beginning," he whispered quietly. Quickly, and as though he had practiced it many times, he knelt down and placed his head on the floor in the corner of the room. Kicking his feet up above him, he balanced himself on the top of his head with heels against the wall. With a sudden twist and tilt of the head, the weight of his body came crushing down. The crack of his neck breaking was the last thing he ever heard.

SAMUEL AWOKE, his head snapping up from his pillow. He was soaked in sweat, breathing in short gasps. His eyes darted around the small bedroom, desperate to assure himself that he was indeed there. He brought a hand up to the back of his neck and rubbed it gently. With a shaking hand he reached over and turned on the bedside lamp. He swung his feet out of the twin-bed and onto the floor. His heart pounding, he stepped across the room, sat down in front of the computer on the desk, and pressed the "on" button.

Waiting, he buried his face in his hands. "That was too, damn real," he said aloud. When the computer came up, Samuel went directly to the internet browser. There he searched and found a World War II veteran's data archive. In the search box titled "Rank and Name" he typed, "Captain Steven Darnell." The image of a photo slowly downloaded onto the screen. Samuel's heart leapt into his throat, his eyes widened in recognition and horror. "Oh, God!" he said. It was him, the man in his dream.

Calvin was sitting at the kitchen table, reading, and absentmindedly eating a bowl of cereal; the box with a large, cartoon of a smiling rabbit was on the table next to him. He didn't notice Samuel enter from the hallway.

Samuel looked at the clock over the stove. "Are you off today?" he asked.

"Uhh—yeah," Calvin answered. "What's up?"

Reaching forward, Samuel grabbed the back of a chair, turned it around, and sat with his elbows on the top of the seat back. Folding his hands together, he looked directly into Calvin's eyes. "You remember when we used to bury things in your backyard, like when your dog Poopers died?"

"Yeah . . . ," Calvin said cautiously. A smile came to his face. "Then we turned around and dug him up six months later to see what his bones looked like." His smile slowly turned to a frown. He looked uncertainly at the spoonful of cereal and milk that was poised in front of his face. "Gee, thanks for bringing that up when I'm eating, Sam," he said and dropped the spoon back into the bowl.

"No problem, man," Samuel said. "And, ahhh . . . well, there's something else I want to dig up."

DR. MILLER'S EYES WERE INTENTLY FOCUSED on the sonogram image on the screen as her hand moved the transducer across Rebecca Kibbling's abdomen. "Your baby is growing nicely," she said. "Everything . . . looks good." She looked at the patient and smiled.

Rebecca eyes twinkled with excitement. "Can you tell?" she asked.

"Yes, I can," the doctor said playfully. "Are you sure you want to know, or would you like to wait?"

"Please. I'd really like to know. Is it a boy or a girl?"

The doctor smiled. "You, Rebecca, are going to have a little girl," she said.

The smile left Rebecca's face and the air seemed to go out of her before she quickly smiled again. "Oh—that's—wonderful," she said. For the rest of the session she didn't say anything to the doctor beyond polite, brief, necessary replies while smiling weakly and averting her eyes.

After dressing and collecting her things, Rebecca went out into the lobby, made a follow-up appointment, and left the office. In the hallway of the medical building, she squinted through watery eyes as she walked quickly towards the exit. As she put a hand on the handle of the glass, exit door she saw them waiting in the parking lot, standing in their white shirts and black ties. They were always there, always watching, following, protecting her.

Rebecca stopped herself; her hand went to the small swell of her stomach. She slowly backed away from the door and looked around. There was an exit sign at the other end of the long hallway, as she walked toward it she pulled her cell phone out of her purse.

Far out at the edge of the parking lot, Nick sat in his car watching the entrance of the building. He's positioned himself so that he could see Rebecca's blue Nissan. She was parked far closer in, but several rows away from the building entrance. The figure of a woman with a kerchief covering her head, suddenly appeared from a passageway at the side of the medical building. The kerchief and the lowered head allowed only a brief glimpse of her face.

"Damn it," Nick said, striking the steering wheel with the palm of his hand. "What are you so afraid of?" As he watched, she walked quickly in a direction away from where her car was parked. In front of the adjacent building, she ducked into a waiting taxi. Nick started his car and followed.

CHAPTER SEVEN

TIMOTHY GODWIN FOLLOWED NATHAN KIBBLING down a hallway in the university's anthropology building. Under his arm, Timothy carried the bulging briefcase. "I really do appreciate your help on this, Nathan," he said. "After what I was told about the potential value I've grown even more anxious to know their meaning."

"Well," Nathan said, "I'm just as curious as you are to know how they'll translate. Professor Eldridge is one of the finest in the field of linguistics." They stopped at an open office door. "Not to mention ancient and dead languages. I'm sure you won't be disappointed." Kibbling put out a hand to usher Timothy in. "Please, after you," he said.

Stepping into the office, Timothy's eyes widened to see Tasha Eldridge, the beautiful dark-haired, professional woman who he'd met at his last book signing. She was sitting behind her desk, reading through a stack of reports and writing notes. As Timothy approached, her eyes came up. After a second she smiled at Timothy in surprise and recognition.

"Dr. Eldridge," Nathan said, "I'd like you to—"

"No introduction is necessary, Nathan," Tasha said. Standing, she reached out to shake Timothy's hand.

"*You're* Professor Eldridge?" Timothy asked.

"Please, I'd prefer to be called Tasha."

"You know one another?" Nathan asked in surprise.

"She came to one of my signings," Timothy said.

Nathan looked thoughtful then his eyes lit up. "Ahhh, I see," he said. "I shouldn't be surprised? Well, Tasha, you could very well be the only person that possesses a signed book from the both of us."

"Then we should be flattered and delighted," Timothy said.

"Indeed," Tasha said with a big smile.

The three of them laughed for a moment before Tasha spoke again. "So what brings you here, Timothy?"

Timothy looked to Professor Kibbling, the professor held out a hand to him indicating he should speak. Taking a breath and letting it out slowly, Timothy began. "Well, in hopes that you can keep a secret." He set the briefcase on her desk. "We'd like to see what you might know about these." The top of the old, overstuffed, heavy leather briefcase almost burst open when he flipped the latches. Timothy gave her an embarrassed smiled and began working out one handful at a time and piling them on the desk.

Staring at the stack of documents, Professor Eldridge's eyes went wide and her mouth fell agape. She looked up at Nathan and then at Timothy. Her hand reached out and very gently touched the edges of the papers. "My God!" she said, "do you have any idea what you have here? . . . No," she said, answering her own question, "or you wouldn't stuff them in a briefcase and handle them like they're old newspapers." She gave both men a chastising look. "I can tell at a glance from the type of paper, the papyrus, and . . . my God, vellum."

"Vellum?" Timothy questioned.

"Yes, vellum," she said," it comes from the Latin word "vitulinum," which means "made from calf," She opened a desk drawer, removed a pair of white gloves and began working them onto her hands. "It was widely used in the sixteenth century. What you have here, *gentlemen*, are great antiquities no matter what's written on them." She sat back down at her desk and began reading silently from the top document. Timothy and Nathan looked at each other and settled into chairs. They watched as Tasha carefully sorted through the documents. As she worked, she spoke as though speaking to herself. "Latin—Greek—Hebrew—Aramaic. I can't believe this collection." She glanced up sternly at Timothy and said, "Where did all this come from? They weren't stolen from the Vatican or something, were they?"

"No," Timothy said with a nervous laugh. He squirmed in his seat and leaned forward. "At least, not that I'm aware of."

Tasha's eyes were back on the manuscripts. "Whoa—," she said. "Oh, my—" With great care, almost as though in reverence, she held up a document that had turned brown-yellow with age. "This parchment," she said, looking meaningfully first at Timothy then at Nathan, "is written in Sumerian."

"Are you sure?" Nathan asked.

"Oh, yeah, I'm certain of that."

Timothy looked from one professor to the other, confusion in his eyes. "Sumerian?"

"This could be thousands of years old. Perhaps 2000 BC, maybe earlier," Tasha said. "But—it doesn't make any sense. Sumerians wrote on clay tablets, over five-thousand years ago. For it to be written on parchment doesn't fit. It was a dead language, long before parchment was first used. How is that possible and why would someone use a language that no longer existed?" She laid the parchment back on the desk and spent several minutes examining it, a gloved finger moving along the written lines. "This must be some kind of religious text. It describes two rebirthing souls bound to earth."

Nathan stood quickly and glared at Timothy. "Well, if you're going to plagiarize someone's work," he said, "I guess it's best that it's from an author that no one knows ever existed." He started toward the door.

"Nathan . . . , you don't understand," Timothy blurted.

The professor stopped at the door and turned around. "What I understand is that you hid behind the facade of being a novelist when you could have honestly published your findings."

"Nathan, it's not that simple," Timothy pled.

"Well, you've made it as simple as you could for yourself. Haven't you?" Nathan said as he stormed off down the hallway.

"What? . . . I didn't know," Timothy exclaimed. He turned to Tasha. She starred at him with questioning eyes.

IT WAS AFTER ONE IN THE MORNING when Calvin's battered Ford Explorer pulled off the highway that ran west through the Florida panhandle, into the parking lot of a convenience store. It was a small and rundown with only two gas pumps. Aside from the clerk visible through the front window, the place looked deserted. Stopping next to the gas pump, Calvin got out and, yawning, arched his back, and stretched out his arms. Samuel got out of the passenger side and walked around the vehicle.

"Ohh, jeez," Calvin said, "why didn't you tell me this little adventure of yours was in Alabama?" Calvin pulled out a credit card from his wallet and put it into the slot on the pump.

Samuel grinned at him. "Because I knew if I told you, you wouldn't have wanted to go."

"You're lucky I don't work tomorrow, Sam, or I'd been really pissed off right now," Calvin said as he set the pump and lifted the nozzle out of its holster.

"Well, I can't do this without you, Cal," Samuel said. He walked up to Calvin, gave him a big smile and patted him on the back. "I don't know how to drive."

"Lucky me," Calvin said wearily.

"But I can't say it looks all that hard," Samuel said, teasing as he walked towards the convenience store.

"Just stay away from my keys," Calvin yelled.

"Want a drink," Samuel called over his shoulder.

"Yeah, Sam, one of those orangeade thing-ees. Get the big one."

Inside the dingy story, Samuel nodded at the sleepy-eyed clerk, walked down the aisles, and picked up a couple of bags of chips and some candy bars. He was at the drink machine, filling two large cups when the bell above the store entrance rang. Looking up he saw Calvin walk in and go up to the counter. Only a moment later the bell rang again. Samuel casually glanced toward the door. A man in torn jeans, a dirty looking t-shirt, and a ski mask pulled down over his face rushed in. He had a revolver in his hand and pointed it a Calvin, then at the clerk, and back again.

"Get on the floor!" the man screamed at Calvin. His dark eyes blazed, crazily through the holes in the mask.

Calvin, his eyes wide in terror, sank quickly and went face down, spread-eagle on the tile floor.

The man turned the gun to the clerk who standing, trembling with his hands up. "Empty the register! All of it!" the robber yelled and threw a plastic bag on the counter. "Try anything stupid and I'll blow your ass away!"

Samuel watched unnoticed. Staring at the back of the gunman's head, he slowly set down the drinks. Quietly, he began to walk towards the robber. When he was only a few steps away, the gunman whirled around and leveled the gun at Samuel's head.

"Get back, man!" the gunman shouted. "Tryin' to sneak up on my ass! I'll shoot you, man!"

Samuel felt anger and adrenalin surge through his body. His stare, locked on the robber's eyes, sharpened and deepened.

"You stupid mother . . . ," the gunman yelled almost in a shriek. "fu—"

Before the robber could spit out another word, Samuel shot out a hand and snatched the pistol. He shoved the man hard in the chest, sending him crashing into the counter and falling to the floor. Standing over the robber, he grabbed him by the front of his shirt, and pulled his body up a few inches off the floor. Cocking the revolver, Samuel put the muzzle on the bridge of the man's nose. "You still have a chance to have a life, Eddie," he said, his voice steady, emphatic, "get off the crack, get a real job, and take care of your wife and two kids." He jerked the robber's shirt and pressed the gun harder. "I won't give you a second chance." He let go of the man and stepped back.

Eyes wide, the robber got up quickly, almost stumbling on shaky legs. He looked at Samuel with wary disbelief, hesitated for a flash before he ran, headlong, crashing into the door. Then, he was gone.

Samuel looked down at the gun in his hand and felt his knees tremble. Calvin got to his feet and both he and the clerk stood staring at Samuel with their mouths open.

It took a minute for the clerk find his voice. "You . . . you know him?"

"He won't be back," Samuel said, as he stuck the gun in the front of his pants. "What do we owe you for the fountain drinks and the snacks?"

"On the house, man," the clerk said.

"Thanks," Samuel said. He looked at Calvin. "Can you get our stuff?"

Calvin nodded; his mouth was still open in astonishment. He watched Samuel walk out the door and cross the parking lot toward the Explorer. Calvin went back to the fountain machine and picked up the drinks and snacks. Trying to hurry after Samuel, he looked at the clerk, shrugged and quickly walked out of the store.

Getting in the driver's seat Calvin placed the fountain drinks and snacks in the middle console. Samuel was bent over, hugging himself, his whole body was trembling. "Man, are you okay?"

"Can we just go?" Samuel asked.

"Sure—sure, Sam," Calvin reassured him. "What just happened in there?"

"Please, Cal, just go, will ya'?"

Calvin started the SUV, and pulled out onto the highway. He drove for a half hour, turning every so often to look at his friend.

Finally, Samuel caught his glance. "I'm okay, Cal, he wasn't going to shoot anyone," he said.

"And how could you know that," Calvin said, squinting back at the road. "Let alone what his name was!"

Samuel picked up the revolver from his lap and slid it underneath his seat. "I usually get it right."

Calvin gave him a quizzical look. "Get what right?"

"You know the finger trick?"

"Yeah," Calvin said.

"Well, as my nightmares got worse, I got better at it."

"What is that supposed to mean?"

Samuel could hear the frustration in his voice. He didn't want to tell him the secret he had kept to himself for so many years, but now he felt the time had come to give Calvin an explanation. He knew he could trust him with the truth, but wasn't sure how he would react. He took a deep breath. "Sometimes . . . ," he said, "I can look people in the eye and know what they're thinking." He could see Calvin didn't believe him. "Alright, Cal. Think of a color."

"You mean—?"

"Yeah, see if I can't tell you what it is."

Calvin looked at his Samuel, concentrating.

"Red—green—yellow," Samuel said with a smile. "Would you make up your damn mind?"

Calvin looked at the road for a second then back at Samuel's eyes.

"Pink," Samuel said. "Are you done?"

Calvin was speechless and could only stare at Samuel for several seconds with his brow knotted. Suddenly, they were both startled by the loud, frantic rattle of stones bouncing up into the fender as the front, right tire veered off onto the shoulder.

"Look out!" Samuel shouted.

Calvin swerved back onto the pavement. With the violence of the correction the tires screeched and the Explorer rocked left then right. Both he and Samuel exhaled in relief when the vehicle was finally under control.

"Maybe I should drive," Samuel teased.

"Like I said, don't touch my keys, Sam."

They laughed.

"I can't believe you can do that!" Calvin said excitedly. "Can you do it anytime you want?"

"Pretty much."

Calvin turned to Samuel with a concerned look. "Ahh . . ."

"Don't worry, Cal," Samuel said, I've learned not to make a habit of it. It's hard to have friends . . . or parents for that matter . . . when you know too much."

"What about that guy in the store—Eddie? You could have got yourself shot."

"He wasn't gonna shoot anybody."

"Jeez, he could have changed his mind."

Samuel shook his head. "If he shot anyone it would have been an accident."

"Well, accidents *do* happen, you know."

Samuel only smiled to himself; he didn't want to put more on Calvin than he felt he needed to know.

"Oh, man!" Calvin said, his face brightening with inspiration. "You know what! You know what we ought to do?"

"What's that?"

"Vegas, baby!"

Samuel rolled his eyes. "You gotta be twenty-one to play in Vegas."

"Oh, yeah," Calvin said, deflated. "Maybe we could—"

"No, Cal," Samuel said. He playfully punched Calvin on the shoulder.

They looked at each other and smiled.

"Hey, I'm just saying . . . ," Calvin started.

"That isn't what all this is about," Samuel said, cutting him off.

"Then what is it all about?"

"That's what we're gonna find out," Samuel said solemnly, staring ahead at the highway that ran toward Alabama.

CHAPTER EIGHT

PROFESSOR ELDRIGE'S FACE was illuminated by the reflecting glow of a single desk lamp, in her otherwise darkened, university office. Her head down, knotted in concentration, she examined one of the ancient documents on her desk.

On a chair next to her Timothy watched, biting his lip nervously. "Thanks for sticking with me on this and working so late," he said.

Distracted from her concentration, Tasha looked at him blankly for a second before she spoke. "I'll be honest with you, Timothy. I am curious as to where these came from but I'm far more curious at the moment to know how they'll translate." She paused, her eyes searching his face. "Don't worry," she continued. "Believe me, Nathan will come around. He'll understand. And he's bound to be just as curious as we are."

"I hope you're right," Timothy said. He looked down at the desk and motioned with a hand. "I wouldn't be where I am today, if it wasn't for him."

Tasha gave him understanding smile.

"So, why did you learn to read Sumerian?" Timothy asked.

"A lot of history has been lost to the world, Timothy. I wanted to try to get some sense of what we've lost. Sumerian is the oldest, known, written language and, I figured, if you want to know history—no better place to begin than when it was first written." Tasha pursed her lips for a moment and gave him an examining look. "Frankly, there is something bothering me."

Timothy's blinked, and adjusted his glasses. "What's that?" he asked.

Tasha leaned back in her chair, staring at him. "A lot of this reads like your book. I thought you couldn't translate any of this."

"I can't," Timothy said, openly meeting her stare. He leaned in, resting his elbows on his knees. "But apparently someone could. Along with these there were a substantial number of handwritten documents in French and German. I translated those, the best I could. Most of the time, the translations were broken up in general phrases—bits and pieces. I just tried to put things together and built my story on them."

"Well," Tasha said. Straightening up in the chair, she pointed to a document on the desk, "here is something that isn't in your book." She glanced at Timothy. "This part of the script reads more like an expository text rather than a narrative. But it's broken up—kind of like it was written in random thoughts, much like what you were saying." She began to read. "The reborn souls have no memory of their previous lives, unless they pass shadows from the past."

"Shadows from the past?" Timothy asked. "What could that be?"

"Shadows. I don't know. Something they see. "Something that . . . that would trigger a memory."

Timothy thought for a moment. "Like a photo?" he asked.

"Yeah, but you're forgetting when this was written, there was no such thing. But, perhaps an item of some kind, or familiar place." Tasha shrugged and shook her head. "This manuscript is very cryptic. And now, it continues using symbolism, saying 'They will know one another by the eyes of fire, the burning beyond the skin, the end is near, a time for a . . . new beginning.' The only one who could know what that meant would be the one who wrote it. That's the trouble with symbolism. It is left to a range of interpretation, rather than direct translation. "

On into the evening, Tasha continued translating, making notes. From time to time she gave Timothy the gist of what was being said and any relevant, historical background she could provide. At one point, in the midst of translating aloud, Tasha read, "'For those to whom death never falls, that are not unlike the devil, '" She gave Timothy a look of intrigue, then continued, "'shall be bound by chains and shackles of iron, to be free no more.' Wow, that's intense. You have got to use that in your next book. Nathan is really missing out. This reference ties into the Bible, centuries before it was written."

"The Bible? How's that?" Timothy asked.

"In the book of Revelations," Tasha answered. "It says that an angel comes down from heaven with a great chain and binds the devil, throwing him into a bottomless pit for a thousand years, and let loose again. But, in this text, those that never die, assuming it means incarnates—those that are evil—are chained up and never let loose." Glancing at the clock on the wall she grimaced and slumped into her chair. "Oh, great," she said rubbing her eyes with both hands. "It's after ten and I've got class at eight tomorrow morning."

"No, please, stop," Timothy said, "I've put you out enough."

Tasha swiveled in her chair and started carefully placing the documents on a shelf in a cabinet behind her desk. "They'll be okay here," she said. "After my classes tomorrow, I'll get back to them," she said.

They left, walking out together into the night air and toward the building's parking lot.

"I'll need at least a few days just to get a general assessment of what's left," Tasha said.

"Please. No rush, I have a signing to do at Brader's Books tomorrow evening."

Tasha suddenly stopped, turned and looked Timothy in the eye.

"What now?" he asked.

For a long moment she studied his face with a frank expression before she answered. "You don't come across to me as being a thief or stupid . . ."

"Well," Timothy said with a weak, embarrassed smile, "thanks for that, I guess."

She started walking again. "I also really enjoyed reading your book."

"Well, that's good to know," Timothy said following behind.

"But, I have to say, I didn't like the ending very much."

"And, why is that?"

"You don't tell who the journeymen really are. You just set up a good ending, for writing another book."

"Well, that's the whole idea in writing a series. Isn't it? You don't tell everything."

"I'm not asking for everything. I just want to know who they are." Tasha looked back at Timothy, her look demanding an explanation.

Timothy stopped walking and averted her eyes. He pursed his lips tightly and cocked his head to one side, but said nothing.

Tasha came a step closer, staring at his eyes. "You really don't know who they are. Do you?" she said.

Timothy shook his head. "No. I don't."

"So, you published a story, not knowing how it ends?"

"Yes."

"How can you not know the ending to your own story?" she asked. "It is your story . . . isn't it?"

Timothy exhaled heavily, blowing air out of his mouth. "Yes," he said, "but not entirely. *The Journeymen Diaries* are based on other writings that are very similar to the ones you're helping me with." He shook his head. "Maybe, Nathan was right and I should have just published the findings of the manuscripts. But that's not what I've done. And now, I am responsible, under contract, to write a second book. All I'm asking is that you keep helping me with the translations and I won't bother you with this any further."

"I don't know what's going on," Tasha said, as they resumed walking. "How on earth did you get those manuscripts? And . . . I'm not so certain I really want to know. But, for you to have possession of them . . . it's like . . . well, it's like someone on the street having the Dead Sea Scrolls under their mattress."

"Are they really that important?" Timothy asked.

"There are very few writings found in the world as significant, Timothy. If they don't belong to you—whoever they *do* belong to . . . ," she said, "you can bet they'll want them back." They reached the parking lot and she turned, walking towards her car. "Goodnight, Timothy," she called.

"Goodnight," he said. He stood watching her walk away.

CALVIN SLOWED THE EXPLORER and eased onto the shoulder of the road.

"Stop here," Samuel said, pointing to the side of the road.

Braking to a stop, Calvin craned his head close to the windshield so that he could see the sign that arched over a closed, iron gate. He read it aloud, "'Stone Creek Cemetery.' A cemetery, Sam?" Calvin said in disbelief. "Are you out of your friggin' mind?! This isn't like digging up a dog!"

Samuel didn't want to say anything. There was too much to try to explain and he didn't really know any of the answers, beyond knowing he had to do it. He pulled the revolver out from underneath the seat, opened the passenger door, and stepped out into the dark, warm night. Above the sound of the Explorer's idling engine, the night was filled with the chirping racket of tree frogs and insects. "Kill the lights and pop open the back, will ya'?"

"You're the one with the gun," Calvin grumbled, sarcastically. "Do you really want to take that with us?"

"Yes, I do."

"Why?" Calvin asked, watching Samuel step out of view.

"Because, I feel safer with it. Let's just leave it at that. Okay?"

"Whatever."

By the time Calvin got to the back of the SUV, Samuel had pulled a sheet off of the tools he'd brought along. There were shovels, flashlights, and a pair of bolt cutters. He picked up the bolt cutters and looked at Calvin in the dim light of a clouded full-moon. "I'll open the gate and you pull inside. I need to find where Steven Darnell is buried."

"Steven, who?"

"Darnell. Steven Darnell," answered Samuel.

"You're really serious about this. Aren't you?"

"Yeah, Cal. I'm doing this with or without you. I have to."

"Okay," Calvin said less than enthusiastically. "This is like got to be against all kinds of laws, Sam. Like we could end up in some redneck jail forever. Who the heck is Steven Darnell and why do you want to dig him up?"

Samuel closed the back hatch of the SUV. He faced Calvin. "I remembered his name after having a dream about him. I looked him up on the internet and found out he really existed. He's—"

"Buried here," Calvin interrupted.

"Yeah."

"Okay, he existed—or at least *did* exist—that's pretty freaky. But, why do you want to dig the guy up?" Calvin asked in exasperation.

"Because, there might be something buried with him, Cal."

"Like *what*?" Calvin asked.

Samuel took a breath, put a hand on Calvin's shoulder, and spoke slowly and calmly. "I don't know, but I need to find out if I'm right."

"Okay, let's see if I got this right," Calvin said, almost sputtering in frustration. He began to count off on his fingers as he spoke. "You *don't* know if anything is buried with him and—*if* there is something—you have no idea what it could be. All of this because of a dream? This is crazy, Sam. If we get caught—we're going to jail."

"Cal, *if* we get caught—just tell them that I was just released from an institution and that I told you that I would kill you if you didn't help." Samuel said. He pulled the revolver out from under the back of his shirt and wiggled it the air.

Calvin threw his hands up in frustration. "Is that supposed to make me feel any better, Sam? You know I'm not gonna do that." Mumbling to himself, Calvin got back into the Explorer.

Samuel walked to the gate and cut the chain that padlocked the iron gate. A minute later, the gate swung open and Calvin drove into the cemetery.

Inside, Samuel led the way, walking in front with a flashlight, guiding the SUV. He directed Calvin along the drive that ran toward the back of the cemetery. They came to a large mausoleum and, after some heated discussion, managed to get the vehicle behind it. With the vehicle out of sight from the road, they each took a flashlight and a shovel, separated, and began searching for Darnell's tombstone.

After a half hour, complaining through much of it, Calvin's light illuminated a mossy, unkempt, marble stone. He read the script aloud to himself, "Captain Steven Darnell, 3rd Armored Division, February 10th, 1915, July 19th, 1945." He swallowed and read it again, silently, to make sure. "Sam," he called out softly, "I think I found him."

Samuel made his way over and stood in front of the stone. He felt a wave of trepidation in seeing a real-world connection to the horrors that haunted him.

"He died right near the end the war," Calvin said.

"Yeah, you found him," Samuel said, taking a deep breath.

"I don't know if I can do this, Sam. This is really creepy." Calvin said. His face was an ashen white in the light reflected off the tombstone.

"You have no idea," Samuel said. "Just help me get down to the casket. I'll take it from there."

"Did this guy die in your dream?"

"Yeah," Samuel said. He drove the point of the shovel into the earth with his foot.

"How?"

"Well, uh . . . he . . . broke his own neck."

TASHA STOOD AT THE FRONT DOOR of her home, searching through her purse. Tired and bleary eyed from a long work day and a long night of deciphering Timothy's documents, she was trying to find her house key by the dim light over the door. Finding it she slid it into the lock. Just as she turned it, a shadowy figure stepped up behind her. Hearing footsteps, she jumped and turned around. She fell back against the door in terror.

"Tasha," a soft, female voice said.

"Oh, my god . . . ," Tasha said, breathlessly. "Rebecca? You nearly gave me a heart attack."

"I'm sorry," the young woman replied and came closer, into the light. Her eyes were red and swollen, and her cheeks smeared with streaks of mascara.

Tasha's mouth fell open. "What's wrong, honey?" she asked.

"I didn't know where else to go," Rebecca whimpered apologetically.

"Oh, no," Tasha said sympathetically, putting her arms around the girl, "please, please come in."

Tasha sat the girl on her sofa and went into the kitchen to make some tea. With the kettle on, she went to the hall closet and walked back to the living room with a blanket. Rebecca was sitting motionless on the edge of the cushion, hugging herself with her arms, her face frozen in hopelessness.

"Here, sweetie," Tasha said, draping the blanket over the girls shoulders. She knelt down in front of Rebecca, reached out, held her hands, and looked up into her eyes. "I need you to tell me what happened," she said gently. "Is the baby okay?"

Rebecca's big eyes rolled open, she nodded, sniffling.

"Honey, is all of this because of the father?"

The girl looked down and said nothing.

"Who is he, Rebecca?" Tasha bent her head lower to try to see into the girl's eyes. "Why won't you tell me who he is," she implored. Your father has—"

Rebecca pulled her hands free and stiffened in fear. "No, don't tell him where I am. Don't tell anyone!"

Tasha stood and sat next to her. She put an arm around her and a hand on hers. "Why? He's your father. Honey, you have to give me a reason."

"They," Rebecca spoke between sobs, "wanted a . . . boy."

Her mouth opening in shock, Tasha said, "Please don't tell me that you're supposed to be a surrogate mother."

Rebecca looked at her and started sobbing hysterically. Tasha held her tightly and let her cry. After awhile, when she felt the tension leave the girl's body, she got Rebecca to her feet and walked her into a spare bedroom. She laid her down and held her hand. Exhausted, the girl fell asleep very quickly.

Finally alone, Tasha settled on the couch with a glass of merlot. No sooner did she touch the wine to her lips when she was startled by two, soft knocks on the door. Her eyes went to the door, then to the clock over the TV; it was after midnight. She got up slowly and tiptoed to the door, her fingers went over the deadbolt, making sure it was set. Her eye went to the peephole. A tall, young man with red hair was standing on her step. His head turned to look down one side of the house and then the other, his body fidgeted up and down as though he was impatient. As she watched, his hand came up towards her and he knocked again, harder this time.

"What do you want?" Tasha demanded, her mouth close to the closed door.

"I'm sorry to bother you so late, ma'am, I'm a friend of Rebecca's and I really need to speak to her. Could you please let her know I'm here? My name is Nick."

"I think you have the wrong house. I don't know a Rebecca."

Nick shook his head. "I know she's in there. I saw that you let her in less than an hour ago. So, please just go get her. It's really important that I see her or I wouldn't be bothering you. Please, lady."

Tasha's face contorted in anger. "What are you doing watching my house? You need to turn around and leave this second!"

"You don't understand!" Nick held his open hands up in pleading and his voice took on an urgency. "We went to school together. Her father—something's not right. He won't let me talk to her either. I was her boyfriend three months ago and, all at once, she's terrified and I can't find out anything."

"If you are not gone by the time I get to the phone I'm calling the police." Tasha said.

"Ma'am, look," Nick said, "she has men following her, and she's afraid of them."

"I'm calling the police," Tasha said. She stepped away from the door and picked up her cell phone, from the coffee table.

The desperation in Nick's voice came through the door. "Why is she being followed? Who's she involved with? What do they want with her?"

Tasha stood frozen with the cell phone in her hand. There was only silence. Cautiously she stepped back the peephole. Nick was still standing at the doorway. In seconds, he backed up, threw his arms up into the air, turned, and walked away. Near the end of the walkway he stopped and looked back, then started away again, crossed the street and disappeared from view.

Tasha made her way back to the couch. She sat hugging her knees, her hand still held tight to the cell phone. It was an hour before she was calm enough to fall sleep.

CHAPTER NINE

SAMUEL AND CALVIN, SWEATING profusely and breathing hard, stood shoulder deep digging in the open grave. There was an audible "thunk" and Samuel felt his shovel hit something solid. The two looked at each other for a second before Calvin scrambled out of the hole.

Samuel worked quickly, he was desperate to see what it was he was so driven to find. Scraping with the shovel, he cleared enough dirt away to where he could see the weathered and decaying wood of the coffin. He stood catching his breath for a second before he raised the shaft of the shovel straight up. Holding it with both hands, he rammed the point down into the wood with all his strength. The top splintered and, after a few more blows, Samuel was able set the shovel aside and rip out the rest of the top with his hands. He tossed the chunks of wood over his head and out of the grave.

When the pieces stopped flying, Calvin saw Samuel bend down out of sight. Morbid curiosity overcame his fear and he cautiously walked up to the edge of the open grave. Suddenly, Samuel stood and raised a canvas, olive-drab, army bag over his head. Startled by the movement rising from the grave, Calvin stepped back. Stumbling over his own feet, he fell to the ground, and then jumped up just as quickly.

"Jesus, Sam, don't do that, will, ya'? Is that what you were looking for?" he asked.

"I hope so," Samuel said. He felt a sense of calm, something of a vindication for all the frenzied haunting of his life, for all the people who told him he was mentally ill or just dreaming.

"Oh, that's right. You didn't know what you were looking for," Calvin said in hushed tone of awe. He looked around furtively, before glancing into the grave. The hollow eye sockets of Captain Steven Darnell looked up into the night sky. The brown, army officer's, dress uniform—now threadbare—draped shapelessly over the bones of his skeleton. "Glad you found what you didn't know you were looking for." His voice was weak, shaky. "So, now can we get the hell out of here?"

"Not yet," Sam said.

Calvin looked up at the sky in desperation and flapped his hands against his sides. "What now?" he said to the stars. He looked back at Samuel. "We stay here much longer, we're gonna get caught and we're gonna go to jail. You have any idea what would happen to guys like us? I don't want some cell mate calling me 'Sweet Cheeks.' You know what I'm sayin'? Now that's a real nightmare for ya'."

Samuel threw the bag aside and climbed out of the hole. "Will you calm down?" he said. "We're gonna leave. But, not before the grave is filled back in. I wouldn't want to be left like this." He picked up the shovel and began refilling the grave. Calvin hesitated, before grabbing his shovel and quickly throwing dirt into the hole.

Twenty minutes later, the Explorer was turning back onto the two-lane and pulling away from the gate. Both Samuel and Calvin were filthy, streaked with brown dirt, sweating, and still breathing hard.

"I can't believe we just robbed a grave," Calvin said. He stepped hard on the gas, squealing the rear tires.

"Cal, we're okay now," Samuel said. "Slow down and take it easy, man."

"Yeah, sorry. I'm okay." He slowed down. "I'm okay."

Samuel turned on the interior cab light, and reached into the bag. He felt a sense of elation when he pulled out a weathered, canvas bound, log book with a U.S. Army insignia stamped on its cover. Hurriedly, he opened the book and turned the pages, his eyes close and squinting in the dim light. He couldn't read it. Page after page, there was nothing but the barest shadow of writing that had long ago been leeched out by moisture seeping into the casket. Disappointed, he laid the book aside.

"What's it say?" Calvin asked excitedly.

"Nothing," Sam said. "There's nothing. It's not legible. The pages are ruined." He reached back into the bag and pulled out a gun, an army issue, forty-five pistol that was caked with rust.

Calvin was sneaking nervous glances while he drove. "Oh, great!" he said sarcastically. "Another gun. You can start a collection."

Samuel paid him no attention, sensing something more than familiar about the rusty pistol. He felt himself getting closer to wherever or to whatever the hellish nightmares were driving him. Gently, he laid the gun on the seat and reached back into the bag. His hand found and pulled out a small object, wrapped in a piece of white, cotton cloth that was now dingy with age. He could feel his heart beat faster and louder, knowing this *was* something he had needed to find. Holding it in the palm of his hand he very slowly, very carefully undid the folds. He hesitated over the last bit before finally uncovering a black sun silver medallion. There was an SS at its center. Staring at it, his eyes seemed to burn inward as though he were leaving the present.

CAPTAIN STEVEN DARNELL STEPPED SLOWLY through the still smoldering ruins of the Wewelsburg castle. A small detachment he'd brought forward followed behind. The light from their flashlights, absorbed by the blackened devastation around them, made it difficult to distinguish anything.

"Sir," Lieutenant Kemuel called, stepping up to him. Darnell didn't respond. Kemuel grabbed the captain by the arm. Darnell turned to look at his lieutenant, his eyes burning with intensity. "There's nothing left here, Steve," the lieutenant said and let go of him. "We received reports from villagers that a small group of SS arrived here, detonated explosives and set fire to what wasn't destroyed. They say they fled in civilian clothing. Locals looted anything that was left. Reports have been sent out."

The captain looked back at the North Tower wall, which appeared to be still intact. Without a word, he began moving toward it.

"Sir, we need to get back to the company and assess the concentration camp situation," the lieutenant called after him. The captain didn't respond. "Steve, what the hell are you looking for? It's all gone."

Darnell stopped suddenly, his eyes focusing on something ahead. It was a door, charred and burned, but still intact. He made his way to it, throwing and pushing any debris out of his way.

Kemuel stood watching him for a second before he shook his head in exasperation and followed.

Darnell turned the door's handle and pushed. It didn't budge. He pushed again, harder. The handle broke free from the brittle burned wood. Throwing the handle to the floor, he reared back and drove his boot into the door with the full force of his weight. The frame splintered with a loud crack. He shoved it open. The beam of his flashlight revealed a narrow, spiraling, staircase leading down into the lower interior of the tower. He looked back at his lieutenant and yelled, "Let's go."

"I'll be damned," said Kemuel.

"Over here," Kemuel ordered the squad, waving them toward him.

Entering the passageway, Darnell led his men down the stairway, into a smoky darkness.

One of the soldiers coughed and grimaced. "You smell that?" he said to no one in particular.

"Yeah," another said, "death. This place gives me the creeps."

"At ease," the lieutenant called behind him.

The cramped, narrow passage of the staircase led them into a large open chamber. The captain pointed his flashlight forward and above, casting light on a large, circular, iron vault. Two spiraling staircases, on either side, led to the top of the vault. The front of the vault was emblazoned with a large, Nazi, black sun symbol. Raising the flashlight beam, he focused it on four large chains suspending a heavy, flat, circular iron lid, its edges frayed with jagged metal. Hanging from the ceiling were red banners, each with a white circle and the Nazi black swastika at the center.

Darnell held up his hand and the line of men stopped. His eyes narrowed as though he were readying himself to meet a great challenge. He began moving again and, after several steps suddenly stopped. His flashlight was fixed on the motionless body of a man lying on the floor. The man wore mediaeval knight's armor, a cloak, and a helmet with a skeletal face shield. The edges of the light led him to another, similarly dressed body, then another —twelve in all. They were next to one another in a row. It looked as though they'd been standing in a formation and died suddenly, collapsing onto the floor together.

"What happened to them?" Lieutenant Kemuel mumbled under his breath as though he were speaking to himself.

"Make sure they're dead," Darnell ordered, "and search them." He moved his light back to the vault, onto the black sun symbol. He knew it meant something, something uncertain—something that frightened him.

Weapons drawn, Darnell's men knelt to the bodies. They were all stiff with rigor mortis. Searching, they removed the head armor; all of them had blond hair and blue eyes. The squad's sergeant held up a small, empty, threaded brass cylinder and its cap. "Sir," he called to Kemuel. He walked over to the lieutenant and handed him the cylinder. "Found this on the floor, next to one of the bodies. None of 'em look like they were shot or anything—no blood or nothin'.""

Kemuel examined it, then held it up to his nose and sniffed lightly. He turned and looked at Darnell across the chamber. "Nothing. I don't smell anything," he said.

"Have them check the others," the Darnell barked.

"You heard the captain, Sergeant," Kemuel said.

"Yes, sir," the sergeant replied.

The soldiers looked carefully around to bodies. Eleven more of the same, empty cylinders were quickly discovered.

"Looks like we got one for each of those armored Krauts, sir," the sergeant said, offering the lieutenant a handful of the cylinders.

"They all had one . . . ,"Kemuel said.

"Cyanide," Darnell said. He turned and headed for the stairs that led to the top of the chamber. Halfway up he saw that the iron-rim edges of the opening were ragged metal, matching the sharp, ragged rim of the plate suspended above. Looking down he moved the beam down into the vault. The muscles of his jaw tightened and a feeling of anger and disgust came to over him.

Kemuel came up beside him and looked down. "Oh, God," he said, covering his nose and mouth from the stench of death.

"God doesn't reside here, Robert," Darnell said.

Below, the exposed body of a young woman was lying on an operating table. There was a long surgical cut above her pelvic area; the gaping wound had been left open.

The two officers descended a steel staircase that led twisting down to floor of the vault.

"Why would they cut her open and just leave her, like that?" the lieutenant asked, his voice shaky.

Searching the rest of the vault with his flashlight, Darnell found the body of a man, lying on the floor against the wall, the hilt of a dagger protruded from his chest. He wore a black, hooded cloak and a silver, skeletal mask covered his face. Around the man's neck was a silver, black sun medallion with SS in its center.

"Who the hell could *that* be?" the lieutenant asked.

Darnell stared at the corpse and slowly moved closer. He lowered himself to his knees and pulled off the mask.

Kemuel was standing beside him looking down. "Is it . . . him?"

"It's hard to tell," Darnell answered, staring at the bloated face. Without consciously thinking about it, Darnell's fingers encircled the medallion and he yanked hard, breaking the silver chain.

"This is sick," the lieutenant said. "Why would they leave her like this? Why'd they kill him?"

Darnell didn't answer. He looked back at the woman on the table. The milky-white skin, the pale-blue, lifeless eyes, wide open, stared directly at him. It was something—something close. He felt a gripping sense of some great, meaningful connection between the two dead bodies. Suddenly, his eyes ablaze with realization, he looked at Kemuel. "It was a Caesarean!" he said.

"What . . . , a baby? There was a child?" Kemuel said, "Jesus, I don't want to know what could have . . ."

Darnell wasn't listening; he jumped to his feet, rushed past the lieutenant and onto the staircase.

"Where are you going?" the lieutenant yelled to Darnell's back as he disappeared at the top of the vault.

Within moments, the captain was running through the ruins and debris of the courtyard. Reaching an unmanned jeep, he jumped into the driver's seat.

"Steve! Steve!" Kemuel shouted running up to him. "Where are you going?"

The captain started the jeep. "No time to explain," he yelled, shifting into gear, he roared off.

In the valley below the castle, Darnell brought the jeep to a skidding stop at the front gate of the Niederhagen concentration camp. American soldiers were directing a mob of newly liberated prisoners toward a line of waiting trucks. He jumped out of the jeep and started moving toward the crowd, his eyes frantically searching the faces.

A sergeant, armed with a Thompson machinegun, was walking towards the captain. "Sir," he called. "Hold up."

Darnell ignored him and moved up to the edge of swarm of emaciated men and women. What was left of their striped, prisoner uniforms was little more than rags. Their haunted eyes—eyes that knew danger—stared hard at the captain. Seeing the size of the crowd, Darnell felt frustration and rage at the impossibility of finding anyone, even if he were to know them when he saw them. In desperation he yelled, "Fleischgeworden!" at the top of his lungs.

Obergruppenfuhrer-SS Henrik, at the far edge of the crowd, stooping as though to avoid notice, whirled around at the sound of the word.

The captain's eye caught the sudden movement of the young, tall, blond, Germanic looking man in civilian clothing. The man's reaction struck Darnell immediately. Unlike the rest of the freed prisoners, he appeared healthy, even robust. Charging into the crowd, he forced his way toward the man. Henrik crouched down further, trying to hide himself amongst the others and move away. The captain shoved through the throng, roughly sweeping away the alarmed and frightened people with his arms.

Squatting down among those around him, Henrik hurriedly removed a small, brass cylinder from his pocket. Twisting open the cap, he removed a small glass vial.

Darnell was on him. Just as he grabbed Henrik, he saw him place the glass vial in his mouth and bite down. The captain tried to shove his fingers into the Nazi's mouth. Henrik struggled against him, clamping his jaw, and turning his head away.

"Damn, you!" Darnell screamed, shaking him violently. "Where is the Fleischgeworden! Wo ist der Fleischgeworden!"

Henrik stopped struggling, and gave him an arrogant smile. Darnell grabbed him by the hair and shook him. Beginning to pant heavily, Henrik's eyes closed tightly and his face began to flush red. Darnell threw him to the ground, leapt down on him and pried his eyes open with his fingers. "Wo ist er?" he demanded. He was only able to look into the man's eyes for a moment before he saw them cloud and roll back into his head. His body began to spasm with death.

"Damn it," Darnell yelled, jumping to his feet. A circle of prisoners and civilians formed around them watching. He searched the faces.

The doctor and the nurse who'd performed the cesarean moved as quickly as they could around the edge of the commotion. The nurse carried the infant that had been torn from the woman's body.

Darnell noticed the nurse, like the dying man, out of place with the glow of health despite her tattered, filthy clothing. She glanced at him fearfully, looked away and put her head down. He could see that she was trying to shield something, cradling it close to her body and turning half away. "You!" he shouted. Frauline, halt!" He pulled the forty-five pistol from his holster and ran after her. The American sergeant and another soldier were almost on

Darnell. He was able to get to the woman before they could get to him. The woman twisted away as he tried to grab at what she held in her arms. There was the anguished cry of an infant.

"Give me the child!" Darnell yelled. "Geben sie mir das kind!"

"Nein! Nein! Nehmen Sie nicht mein kind!"

People from the crowd closed in and tried to help the young woman, yelling, their weakened arms pulled at Darnell. He swung an arm and knocked them off. Shoving the woman to the ground, he put the muzzle of the automatic pistol to the baby's head. One of the pursuing soldiers dove, hitting Darnell with a headlong tackle just as he fired. The loud blast stunned the crowd to silence. Two soldiers wrestled the gun away and pinned Darnell to the ground. The captain raved, screaming madly at the top of his lungs as they dragged him off.

"Sir, you are under arrest," the sergeant yelled, struggling to keep him under control. "Lock him down, he's lost it," he said to his partner.

Lying on the dirt beside them, the nurse laid still, a rapidly expanding blood stain on her ragged tunic, she gasped for her last breaths. The doctor came forward, kneeling down next to her. He picked up the crying infant, cradled it in his arms, and continued toward the waiting trucks.

"SAM! WELL?" CALVIN CALLED louder. "Ya' gonna tell me what that is?"

Samuel turned and looked at Calvin, his eyes focusing slowly like he was coming out of a trance. He blinked and took a deep breath. "It's a black sun . . . ," he said, "an occult symbol used in Nazi mysticism." He held up the medallion and shook it for emphasis. "This was worn by a man believed to have been Reichsfuhrer Himmler."

"Why would it have been buried with Darnell?"

It was the only thing possible, Samuel thought. As crazy as it was, it was the only thing that fit—the only thing that made any sense of all of his madness. He looked at his friend and spoke with his voice shaking in fear at his own words. "It was buried with me—because that's what I told my first lieutenant to do—I told him to bury it with me."

Calvin looked at Samuel. He started a smile, but then his mouth dropped open and his eyes narrowed like he was looking at a mad man. "Excuse me. Could you repeat that?"

Samuel felt sick. It was too much—too much horror, too much pain, and there was too much he had to do. "I was Captain Steven Darnell—in another life," he said.

"Wha . . . ," Calvin said.

"Don't you see, Cal? How else could I have known about something being buried there?" Samuel said. Calvin was giving him the look that people had given his whole life, the look that said there was something very wrong with him.

Calvin's eyes shot back to the road. "Okay—now," he said shaking his head and grunting a nervous laugh. "This is all getting way too weird. You're starting to sound like a journeyman."

"A journeyman?" Samuel said. "What's that?" Calvin turned toward him and Samuel tried to look into his eyes, but he was only able to get a glimpse before his head turned back to the road.

"Ya' know, I've had some good ideas, but this dream thing about Darnell, oh, that's good. Godwin would use it. His book never had anything buried with a dead guy. That's pretty creepy. " He looked over at Samuel's face. "You don't know what I'm talking about—do you?" Samuel was staring at him so intensely that he looked back to the road. "You're doing that thing again, aren't you?"

"A book, Calvin?" Samuel asked. "What book?"

"Yeah . . . ," Calvin said, "would you mind stopping that stare thing, it makes me nervous. Timothy Godwin's, *The Journeymen Diaries.* I don't believe you never heard of it! A big ass best seller! There's these two guys—Victor Wilton . . ."

On hearing Wilton's name a bolt of recognition sent shivers down Samuel's spine.

"And Sebastian Loxton," Calvin continued enthusiastically.

Staring at the dark road ahead, Samuel's eyes glazed over, a scene flashed in his mind with an overwhelming sense of reality. He saw Sebastian Loxton, he saw him riding into a woodland clearing on a horse. He was wearing the red uniform of a British army officer in the revolutionary war era. Shuttering in horror, Samuel shook the vision away.

Calvin was going on. "Both of these guys are incarnates and have fought each other through one century after another. Anyway, Victor hides things in churches and graves so that he can use them in the next life. And . . ."

Samuel raised his hand. "I got it, Cal, I got it. Where's your copy of the book? I want to read it."

"Sure, man. It's at home."

"Do you know where we can get another copy?"

Calvin shrugged. "Just about anywhere."

CHAPTER TEN

THE NEXT MORNING, Tasha peeked into the guestroom, Rebecca was still sleeping soundly. She was curled up under the blanket, her angelic face didn't seem to have a care in the world. Tasha backed out and made her way to the kitchen. She picked her purse up off of the counter and dug out her cell phone. Turning her back to the living room, she dialed.

"Yes," she said softly into the phone, "Nathan. I don't want you to worry, Rebecca's fine. She's here with me . . . yes, the baby is fine too. She's just feeling . . . a little overwhelmed right now. She's growing up way too fast. . . . Just let her stay with me for awhile. Let us have some sister time. Okay? I'll call you once things calm down . . . of course . . . yes, yes . . . Oh, it's my pleasure . . . Okay, bye." She ended the call and, as quietly as possible, set the phone down on the counter. Her eyes rolled up to see Rebecca, standing in the living room, her eyes, wide and fearful, stared at her accusingly.

"Why did you have to call him?" the girl asked.

"Honey, they needed to know where you are. Otherwise they weren't going to stop looking for you," Tasha said, her eyes asking for understanding. "At least this way we have some time to figure out what to do."

"I thought I could trust you," Rebecca said.

"Rebecca, you can. If we didn't tell your parents there would be the police and . . . television—you don't want all that, do you?"

The young woman narrowed her eyes in suspicion, then looked away, and shook her head slowly from side to side.

"Sweetheart, just trust me to make the right decision," Tasha said reaching out for the girl's hands.

Rebecca moved back, away, still shaking her head. "You just don't know . . . you don't know," she said.

CALVIN, WITH SAMUEL FOLLOWING, walked in through the entry door of the first truck stop they'd came to on the rural stretch of highway. He rose up on his toes and looked around the store. The only other customer in the bleak, early morning hour was a haggard, sleepy looking truck driver standing at the counter, scratching off lottery tickets.

"Over there," Calvin said and started walking toward the back. He stopped in front of a long book rack full of paperbacks. His eyes scanned from one end of the rack to the other, before he grabbed what he was looking for. "Here," Calvin said, handing it to Samuel, *"The Journeymen Diaries."*

Holding the book, Samuel felt something of an unsettling nervousness. He opened it to a random page in the middle and began to read. His eyes moved quickly, back and forth, across the type.

"It's worth owning. At least it is to me," Calvin said. Samuel showed no reaction. Calvin laughed. "Gets you pretty quick, Doesn't it?"

"Yeah," Samuel mumbled. What little he'd read had brought an achingly familiar memory crawling straight into his gut.

He looked up from the book and tried to blink the dread from his eyes. "Yes, it does." He closed the book and made himself smile at his friend.

At the checkout counter, while Samuel paid the clerk, Calvin picked up a newspaper and flipped through to the entertainment section. He lit up with delight. "Hey, Sam," he said, tapping a picture over a story on the main page, "this is him, Godwin, the author."

Samuel fixed a hard stare into the pleasant eyes of the smiling Timothy Godwin. "Add the paper, please," he said to the clerk.

On the ride back, Samuel began reading as soon as the oncoming morning allowed enough light. He immediately found himself mesmerized by the book.

For more than an hour the two were silent before Calvin cleared his throat and spoke. "Sam, I was thinking."

"What's that?" Samuel mumbled, his eyes intently fixed on the book.

"Maybe, you shouldn't read that." Calvin said, giving Samuel a look of concern.

Samuel looked up, his penetrating stare fixing Calvin's eyes. After a second, the face softened and he smiled. "Why?"

"Sam . . . , you're already having nightmares. I'm not so sure it's such a good idea."

Samuel could read it clearly. Calvin was trying to come to grips with something impossible to believe; something he was afraid to believe. "Go on," Samuel said, with a nod of his head.

"Jesus, Sam—we just dug up a solder's grave, because of a dream you had. And, that's pretty damn crazy, if you don't mind me saying so. And you *knew*—you *knew* something was buried with the guy. And, I won't lie to you—heck, you'd see through it anyway." Calvin was looking ahead at the road now, his head shaking from side to side. "I'm having a hard time believing, that you're the guy that was buried there." He stopped shaking his head and turned to look at Samuel. "And, if you are, what are you doing here?"

Samuel closed the book. "That's what I've been trying to figure out," he said.

"So, you really believe you were him . . . Captain Darnell?"

"No, Calvin," Samuel said, "I don't believe it . . . I *know* it."

TASHA SAT IN HER OFFICE talking with a student when a figure in the doorway caught her eye. Looking up she saw Nathan Kibbling. She acknowledged his presence with her eyes and raised a finger, signaling him to wait.

"But, Lena, don't worry, we're not going to go much further with the Egyptian contributions in this course," Tasha said to a young student.

The girl's thin body reacted, swaying with relief. "Whew! That's good, Dr. Eldridge. I was—"

The professor smiled at her. "No, you're paper is just fine. Just make sure you read the selections on the Semitic people for next week."

"I've already read it," she said, her voice squeaking.

"Great, see you Monday."

The young lady backed out, almost bowing with her goodbyes. Nathan moved to let her pass and stood watching her walk down the hall. "Let me guess," he said, turning back to Tasha with a sarcastic smile, "a freshman."

Tasha smiled somewhat nervously. "Hi, Nathan."

He came in and stood in front of her desk. "How is Rebecca doing?" he asked.

"She's—okay," Tasha said.

He raised his hands in frustration and started pacing. "I don't understand. When is she coming home?"

"I don't know. Just give me a few more days with her. Let her come home on her own."

"Why didn't she come home after her doctor's appointment?" He looked at her, imploring.

"Nathan, she's frightened . . . and for good reason. Having a baby is an awful lot to handle at her age. Perhaps she didn't want you to see that."

Nathan stopped pacing, sighed and looked up at the ceiling. "Frightened of what? She knows her mother and I are there for her."

Tasha gave him a sympathetic look. "Do you know what Rebecca's plans are once the baby is born?"

"Well," Nathan said, "at the very least to take care of the child, I would hope."

Tasha smiled and nodded. "Like I said, just give me a few more days with her."

"I don't know what else to do," he said. He shook his head and took a step toward the door. "I'll leave it to you for a few days. Thanks."

"Oh," Tasha said with hesitation, stopping him. "There is one thing, I'm not sure if it's important or not, but it brought me some . . . concern. Do you know a young man named 'Nick?'"

Nathan turned and snapped his face to her. His voice was tight and controlled. "How is it that you know Nick?"

"It was bizarre, somewhat frightening really, he showed up at my place in the middle of the night, wanting to talk to Rebecca."

Standing icily still, Nathan's eyes took on an angry cast, but he spoke calmly. "Please tell me you didn't allow it."

"No, of course not. He said he and Rebecca were friends, but she's never mentioned him to me and, well, he gave me the creeps. I'd tell Rebecca, but . . . I don't think she needs that . . ."

"Gave you the creeps?"

"He said things."

"Things? Exactly, what kind of things?" Nathan asked.

"Well, he was somewhat aggressive and almost . . . raving about men that were following Rebecca. He was adamant, wanting to know why, who they were, and what they wanted with her."

Nathan turned away from Tasha. "Interesting," he said. He faced her again. "I'm afraid that's my fault."

"What do you mean?"

"Like with you, he showed up late one evening at my home, wanting to see Rebecca. She'd never even mentioned his name to me. When I asked her about him, she said she knew him from school, but wanted nothing more to do with him. He told me that he '*would*' see her. So . . . , rather than contacting the police, I put someone in charge of looking after her when I or her mother couldn't be with her. Rebecca has far more important things to be concerned with right now. As, I'm sure you understand."

"Is there a chance he could be the father?"

"Please, Tasha," Nathan said, sneering, "can we not discuss this any further, out of respect for Rebecca and the situation she's in. I assure you, I have her best interest in mind."

Tasha nodded in agreement. "Yes, of course."

"If you like, I can see that your home is watched, just in case he shows up again."

"No. No, that's okay. I'm sure things will be fine. I can handle him if he should come back."

"Well, do call me if there is anything I can do to help move things along," Nathan said turning. Halfway out of the office he stopped and turned back to her. "Oh, and I want to apologize for last night. I wasn't at my best. Should you see Timothy . . . would you . . . let him know."

"Why don't you tell him yourself? He'll be doing a signing this evening at The Book House."

"Right, excellent," Nathan said, smiling, "thanks." He left the office.

Tasha smiled to herself and went back to correcting the stack of student papers on her desk.

SAMUEL SAT AT THE SMALL DESK in his room. His eyes were sunken and red from reading, a lack of sleep, and the reawakening of horrors that had been a distant, forgotten part of his being. On his bed a newspaper, open to a full page ad: "*The Journeymen Diaries,* Timothy Godwin, Book Signing, at The Book House." Taped on the walls of the room were pages torn from the book, many sentences and paragraphs marked in yellow highlight. They were placed together in sections he'd organized by the periods of time in which they'd occurred. The haphazard angles in which the pages hung told of the frenzied haste of the project. More torn out pages covered the desktop along with the cover that he'd ripped from the book. Samuel had hardly left the room since he and Calvin returned from Alabama. He'd eaten nothing since starting to read the book on the road. His lips moving, he read very quickly, mumbling silently to help himself believe what the words were actually saying. Holding his place with a finger, he ran a hand around the clutter on the desktop and finally found his yellow marker. He began to highlight a section when he suddenly stopped, realizing that he didn't need to read any further. He raised his eyes to stare blankly, trance like, at the wall as the scene, in all its painful detail, played itself out in his mind.

IN A WOODLAND CLEARING, Victor Wilton and three other colonists were on their knees, their hands tied behind their backs. They were breathing heavily from their unsuccessful attempts to avoid capture; their clothes were torn, mere remnants of what was left of the rough-hewn shirts and pants. Victor intently listened and watched his captors, a squad of British regulars, for any information he might be able to use to help him get back to his wife and children. Standing around speaking in their lower-class accents, they alternately joked crudely about women in America or griped about how unfairly the army treated them. They were anxious to get back to their base where there was better food, a tavern, and, apparently, women to be had if one could come up with a few schillings.

At the sound of horse's hooves pounding from down the trail, the soldiers fell silent. They straightened up and moved away from one another to give the appearance they were indeed closely watching their charges.

Victor's eyes, sharp with smoldering anger, were fixed on the edge of the clearing as though he were expecting some great evil. He had suffered greatly from horrible nightmares since childhood. The dreams persisted, relentlessly haunting him no matter what he did. Somehow the events of the last month, the efforts of the British soldiers at destroying their farms and homes, had crystallized his dreams. Day by day, as the dreams sharpened, they came together and made more and more sense. To his mind they were vindicating what he'd always known: they were more than dreams, they were connected to an ancient cycle that he was a part of. Every fiber of his being was telling him that the purpose of the dreams—what they had been driving him towards his entire life—was about to come before him.

The pounding grew louder, they were moving fast. Suddenly they burst into the clearing. There were three British officers led by a commander on a roan stallion.

"Blimey," said one of the guards to another, "if it isn't Colonel Sebastian Loxton, his-self."

The soldiers came to attention and their sergeant approached as the commander dismounted. "Sir," he said saluting, "these are the captured conspirators."

Commander Loxton never looked at him. "Very well," he said and handed him the reins to his horse. A sinister smile came to his face as he walked slowly up to the kneeling Victor. "Isn't it strange how our paths continue to cross," he said.

Victor's eyes, flaming with hatred looked up at him. The two men locked onto one another with a penetrating stare. Immediately, everything, the endless eons of unspeakable horror, made sense. "Someone has to stop you," he all but hissed.

An amusement crossed Loxton's eyes and he lifted his nose into the air. "Well, it won't be you this time—will it?" He stepped a few feet to his left and stood in front of the next prisoner. "Do you know where this man lives?" he asked, motioning with his head toward Victor. The man lowered his head, ignoring the question. Loxton grabbed the man by the hair and forced his face up. "Look at me!" he demanded, staring into the man's eyes. "Where does this man live?"

With a fierce growl, Victor sprang to his feet and charged into Loxton. He threw his shoulder into the surprised officer and knocked him to the ground. One of the soldiers stepped up and struck Victor in the jaw with the butt of his rifle. He fell, hard, face first on the ground. One of the junior officers pulled a pistol from his belt, held it to Victor's head, and cocked it.

"No! Don't kill him!" Sebastian ordered getting to his feet.

The officer looked at him questioningly, then lowered the weapon. Two of the soldiers grabbed the dazed prisoner, lifted him up to his knees, and restrained him.

Loxton dusted off his uniform and walked back to the man he'd been questioning. He grabbed him by the chin, and looked into his eyes. "Let's try this again, shall we? Does he have any family?"

"No!" Victor screamed. "Don't look at him!"

Though the man said nothing, a sly smile came to Loxton's face. "Thank you," he said, "I think we have our answer." He stepped over to Victor and suddenly lashed out with his fist, striking him squarely in the mouth. Stunned by the force of the blow, Victor's body went limp in the grasp of the soldiers. While shaking the sting from his hand, the commander casually ordered, "Kill them all—all but this one." He nodded at Victor.

The soldiers sprang into action and dragged the other three men to the edge of the clearing. In panic, the men struggled and plead for mercy to the deaf ears of the soldiers. Victor stared up at Loxton with pure hatred in his eyes.

"You're getting to live for the moment," Loxton said.

At the edge of the clearing, one of the men prayed, his voice shaking with fear. "Ready—" called an officer.

Loxton ignored the ongoing execution. "I want you to have some time to think about something," he said.

"Aim . . ."

"What I'm doing to your wife and daughters, while I'm gone."

Furious, Victor struggled against the grip of the soldiers, trying to get at Loxton.

"Fire!" The air exploded with the cruel roar of the muskets.

Loxton only grinned at Victor while working a riding glove onto his hand. "Have him tied to a tree," he ordered to one of the soldiers.

"No!" Victor screamed.

While the soldiers dutifully dragged Victor toward the back of the clearing, Loxton mounted his horse, wheeled around and rode out at a gallop.

In Victor's small, log cabin home, his wife Eileen tended the coals under the kettle that was steaming on the hearth. She wiped her forehead with the back of her hand and looked over at her daughters. She smiled. The girls, Sophia and Serena were sitting on the bed making believe that an old homemade ragdoll was their naughty child. Walking to the cupboard, Eileen took out four wooden plates and placed them on the table. "Sophia, Serena, no more time for play. Help me get dinner ready."

Two hard knocks sounded at the plank door. Eileen and the girls froze in surprise and anticipation; visitors were rare. Wiping her hands on her apron and quickly patting her hair in place, Eileen walked to the door. She blinked in surprise and then smiled politely at the British officer standing on her doorstep.

The officer removed his hat in formal greeting. "Eileen, I believe," he said with a cold glint in his eye.

"Yes?" she asked. Her smile faded at a sudden sense of danger. "Do I know you?"

The man gave her a knowing smile. "Your husband . . . , Victor, sent me," he said, putting a hand up against the door. "May I come in?"

IN THE CLEARING, TWO BRITISH REGULARS stood talking and laughing at their own, crude humor. Behind them, Victor sagged against the tree his arms were bound around. Frantic with worry about his family, his weary eyes darted at every sound, furiously seeking some hope. Suddenly, there was the boom of a large bore muzzle loader. One of the soldiers was spun around from the impact of a musket ball and fell to the ground. There were more shots. Another soldier grasped his side and cursed, "Bloody, hell!" as he too collapsed. An explosion of noise and smoke came from the woods at the clearing's edge. Yelling and screeching war-hoops, several men, all settlers, Victor's neighbors, came charging in with guns, swords, or any farm tool they were able to use for a weapon. The British detachment, many of them dozing, was caught unaware, away from their weapons. Most were cut down where they stood, a few were lucky to be able to run headlong into the woods.

A young man came running up to Victor. He pulled a knife and began cutting his bindings. "It appears we were late," he said.

"You have no idea," Victor told him. "Hurry, I need your sword and a pistol!" He ripped the weapons from the man's hands and, taking off in a dead run, charged into the woods. Heedless of the branches that tore at him, his eyes only saw the way ahead, running and hoping the short cut through the woods would get him home in time.

He ran on, dodging between the trees and brush, before finally crashing out of the woods into the dried stalks of his cornfield. His body aching for breath, he didn't stop until he'd reached the front yard of his cabin. Beyond the sound of his heaving for air, there was nothing. His ears strained, wanting to hear the sounds of life. There was nothing but a great, menacing silence that could only mean one thing. With slow, deliberate steps he walked across the yard. His boots sounded as he climbed the two wooden steps and onto the floor of the porch. Afraid, he hesitated for a moment, then shoved open the front door.

"No," he said quietly, horror drained the color from his face. It was more than he could make sense of. "No," he said again, going to his knees.

SAMUEL FELT THE AGONY OF THAT DAY course through his own body. It was more than mere words. He saw the bodies of his abused, tortured, and slaughtered wife and children. It was more than a story; it was a part of him—a forgotten memory. Buried inside of him, it had haunted his whole life. He couldn't stop the pain or the tears that came to his eyes.

"Yes," he said, highlighting furiously. "I know who you are!" he screamed. Slowly opening his hands, he let what was left of the book fall to his desk. Leaning back in the chair and closing his eyes, he tried to relax in the stillness of the room. There were more pages, but there was no point in reading any further—no point in bringing on more pain. He knew now that the agony would never end for him. Now, there was only what had to be done what he *had* to do. Bending, he slid out the desk's bottom drawer. Reaching inside, he pulled out the revolver he'd taken from the robber.

CHAPTER ELEVEN

TIMOTHY SAT SMILING AT A TABLE stacked with copies of his book. The Book House was brightly lit and yet had a quiet warmth to it. The staff had been friendly and the turnout of eager, buying fans was more than even his agent had hoped for.

"Thank you so much, Felicia," he said as he finished a signing. He looked up, handing her the book, and saw Nathan approaching from across the front of the store. Timothy stood up, and smiled at the next person in line. "Please excuse me for just a moment," he said.

He walked from behind the table and up to Nathan. "I'm surprised to see you here," he said.

Nathan held out his hand. The two shook hands and exchanged friendly, but awkward smiles.

"Well, I had to see how my competition was holding up," Nathan said.

Timothy gave a quick laugh. "I didn't know we were competing." He released his grip from the handshake, but Nathan gripped tighter, holding on.

"Timothy," he said, "I feel . . . I may have been a bit too rash last night. So, I wanted to stop by and apologize."

"You shouldn't apologize at all," Timothy said, shaking his head.

Nathan let go of Timothy's hand.

"If you have time later," Timothy added. "I'd like to explain some things. I'll be finished at eight if you want to stop by."

"I'll be here," Nathan said smiling. "You really should get back to your new livelihood." He gestured toward the line waiting at the table, their anxious faces looking at Timothy.

"Yeah," Timothy said turning toward the table. "I look forward to our meeting."

NICK STRATTON KNELT HIDDEN in the dark, behind the crepe myrtle bushes in Tasha Eldridge's front yard. He had been watching her house for hours, his eyes darting from one window to another at the slightest hint of sound or light. In the time he'd been there, there was only an occasional thump of a door or the switch of a light. It was obvious that someone was home, but nothing that told him if Rebecca was inside.

"Come on," he said softly aloud to himself. "Where are you?"

Getting to his feet, crouching, he ran like a swift, dark shadow across the open yard to the side of the house. There were two windows along the wall. Moving cautiously, he stopped at each, trying to peek in past the blinds. Unable to see anything, he attempted to pry one of the windows open with his fingers, testing it to see if it was locked. It wouldn't budge. Moving to the back corner of the house, he stood stiffly and hugged the wall before taking a quick look into the backyard. A dim, yellow bulb cast a weak light that hardly reached more than ten feet from the backdoor. There was nothing.

Nick rested his hands against the house and looking into the backyard, his eyes caught the movement of a dark shadow slowly moving over him. In sudden shock and fear, he exploded, whirling around. Instinctively, he turned with his fists up, in a fighting stance. He found himself facing the hulking outline of a hooded figure that was even bigger than he was. His eyes went from fierce and angry to round and frightened. A low hiss of breath came from the beneath the hood and, at the same instant, a gloved hand shot out, grabbing his throat.

The iron grip of the fingers dug into Nick's neck from both sides of his Adam's apple. The grip was so tight that Nick could do nothing but put his hands up on his attacker's and hopelessly try to pry the fingers loose. He was only able to mumble a weak, grunting and unintelligible plea. But the fingers only dug deeper. Nick's eyes bulged out, seeming ready to pop out their sockets, and his mumble became a hushed, shuttering whimper. Desperately fighting for his life with his last bit of consciousness, he threw frantic punches at the man's head. There was no response from his attacker who was easily able to ward off the wild blows and tighten his grip at the same time. There were a couple of subdued, little pops as small bones in Nick's neck snapped. It was only a matter of seconds. As Nick's arms fell to his side and his body became still, the attacker reached out with his other hand, held onto Nick's head, and gave a quick, violent twist. In an easy motion he threw the lifeless body over his shoulder, turned and, at an unhurried pace, walked away across the dark yard toward the street where two other hooded figures waited in the dark.

"SAM," CALVIN CALLED OUT, as he entered his apartment. "Sam! Are you here? I'm off early." There was no response or sound. He stood, looking towards the hallway that led to the bedrooms with a quizzical expression on his face. He shrugged and walked down the hall to the door of the second bedroom. Knocking softly, he listened for a response, then turned the doorknob and opened the door. "Sam," he called softly into the dark room. His hand went to the wall beside the door, found the light switch, and flipped it on.

"Holy crap!" Calvin said aloud. Stunned, his body jerking backward in alarm. The walls were covered with pages from a book, the haphazard placements looked like they were slapped up in manic madness. He could see that many of the pages had passages, sometimes whole paragraphs, highlighted in yellow. There was no sign of Samuel. "What the hell is wrong with you, Sam," he said to himself as he moved closer to the wall.

The pages were from two copies of *The Journeymen Diaries*. He read for several minutes, moving from one section of the wall to another. He noticed that some pages were in numerical order, while others weren't. The out of sequence pages were arranged into different groups, seeming to have some connection to the various incarnations of the Sebastian and Victor characters.

Fear began to grip Calvin. "What's going on, Sam?"

Turning, he saw the torn off cover of the book lying on the desk. He picked it up and leafed through the few pages still attached. On the title page was written, "To Calvin, my biggest fan. Thanks, Timothy Godwin."

Calvin's face fell in disappointment. "That's great. Just great," he said. "Damn it, Sam". He slumped to sit on the bed. "Why'd you have to go and do that for? Man. That's great. Just great."

His head turned to the newspaper lying next to him, it was open to an ad for Timothy Godwin's signing at The Book House. Looking down at what was left of his prized volume, he didn't make any reaction at first. Slowly, his eyes widened in realization. He looked at his watch and thought a moment longer. "Oh, no!" he said, jumping to his feet. "Oh, crap!" He raced out of the room.

THE MANAGER OF THE BOOK HOUSE, a pleasant, middle-aged woman, was smiling and shaking hands with Timothy. "For a while there," she said, "I didn't think we'd get you out of here by eight with the crowd that showed up. I really want to thank you for being here, Mr. Godwin."

"The pleasure was all mine. The turnout was great," Timothy said.

"Well, we'll have to make sure you come back after your next release," the manager said.

"I look forward to it," Timothy said. "Thank you."

As she walked away, Timothy sat down at the signing table and began to gather his things. Suddenly startled by a presence, he looked up.

Samuel, wearing a sweat-jacket with his hands in his pockets, was standing a few steps in front of him, staring at him. Desperate to see into Timothy's eyes, his stare burned with a glaring intensity. He quickly stepped up to the table, pulled the gun out of his pocket, and pointed it at the author's head. "Time for a new beginning," he said.

Frozen with fear, Timothy could do little but stare wide-eyed into the face of an incredibly angry young man. The stare continued for terrifying seconds, before Samuel's expression began to break down. The gun in his hand began to tremble as his stare collapsed into doubt and then disbelief.

Samuel lowered the gun. He knew he'd nearly made a horrible mistake. How could he have been wrong? Godwin had to have been the one. It's the only thing that could make any sense of it all. How else could he have known so much?

"No," Samuel said, his voice raw and shaky. With tears coming to his eyes, he backed slowly away a few steps, then turned and ran. He heard the manager scream, "Oh, my, God!" just as he slammed the door open. Running wildly, he cut down an alley that led to the back of The Book House. He ran down past the dumpsters, broken, wooden pallets, and debris behind the other stores along the strip. It was all too much for him, even running at breakneck-speed he knew he couldn't get away from it. Tears flooded down his face. He couldn't stop his mind from reviewing his whole shattered, torturous life. Just when he'd thought that maybe he'd finally found an end to it all, his hopes were dashed back to nothing. He ran on for blocks, crossing side streets, trying to stay behind the stores that lined the main street. Finally, exhausted, he slumped against a block wall and slid down to sit on the pavement behind a trash dumpster.

His chest heaved as he tried to catch his breath. He had to think. There was something, something tickling his memory. Godwin's eyes, wide with fright, kept flashing into his mind. "Who are you?" he said aloud, "I know you from somewhere." He set the gun on ground next to him and covered his face. Rubbing his eyes with his hands, he tried to rub the vision away. But, Timothy's wide, terrified eyes were still there; still there, looking back at him. Something was close, eating into his deepest memories—some deep connection to those eyes. "What is it?"

He opened his eyes and looked up to the night sky. Was he supposed to go on in agony for the rest of his existence? For eternity? What was it that he saw in those eyes that was screaming so loudly at his soul? He tried to focus. Closing his eyes he replayed the whole scene, it flashed into his mind, the bookstore, the terrified eyes, but it was a child sitting there. Everything was just like it happened, him pointing the gun, and it's Godwin, Timothy Godwin, but he's a child of no more than six. He sees himself lower the gun from the face of the terrified, frozen little boy.

Suddenly, Samuel's eyes shot open. It all connected, coming together in his mind. His lips mouthed the name,

"Timothy?" The name and the face of the boy erupted in his mind and his heart.

"Oh, God!" he cried aloud, "Tim!"

He no sooner started to wonder about how Timothy knew so much when it all became obvious.

"Oh, Timothy," he said aloud, "what have you done?"

Staring into the nothingness of the trash strewn alley, he was overwhelmed by the flash of a vision of himself moving through a cemetery. Hot and soaked with sweat, a panic caught in his throat, moving through the dark graveyard, searching. The power of the sensations hit him like a crushing wave. Suddenly, he was in a mausoleum, a death chamber. His flashlight settled on an ironwood chest.

Then, as quickly at it had appeared, the vision was gone. "Yes," he said quietly. "Alexandria." His head fell to his chest in defeat. It was several minutes before he found the strength to stand. He looked up and down the alley. There was no one. He took off the jacket and stuffed it down in a corner of the dumpster. Bending, he picked up the pistol, put it in his waistband, and ran out of the alley.

AS SOON AS HE TURNED THE EXPLORER onto thirteenth, Calvin saw the flashing lights of the police cars parked in front of The Book House. His face registered more regret than surprise.

"Oh, crap," he said.

In front of the store, he slowed and stopped. There were a few people watching from behind the police barricades. He rolled down the window. "Hey, man, what's going on?" he called to a young guy in shorts, sandals, and a university t-shirt.

"Some guy tried to knock off Timothy Godwin," the kid said, sounding proud to be in the know.

Calvin swallowed. "Did anyone get hurt?"

"Nah," the kid said with disappointment, "the guy choked and ran off. They got cops all over looking for him."

"Wow," he said. "Thanks, man."

Calvin pulled away slowly, driving very carefully. Just down the street, a policeman with a dog stood in the road talking to another officer in a patrol car. For blocks, at every crossing road, there were squad cars or cops on motorcycles. While he nervously eyed the police, Calvin tried to look down the alleys and streets between the stores.

As he neared the traffic light on University, Calvin realized he was in the wrong lane. Suddenly, he darted into the left turn lane cutting off a car behind him. The driver gave him an angry, long blast of his horn. "Sorry," Calvin said to himself and waved an apology. "Calm down," he said to himself, "I've got to calm down. Think. Where would you go?"

He drove, criss-crossing the back streets, circling around The Book House, but never getting too close to the bookstore and the police. Guided by nothing more than hunches, he would occasionally dart down side road. After a harrowing, fruitless hour his eyes narrowed in thought. "I wonder," he said to himself. He drove east to the outskirts of town and pulled into the parking lot of a convenience store. He went into the store, bought a large fountain drink, got back into his car, and waited. Sipping at the soda and staring blankly out the windshield, something caught his attention. In the flash of the headlights from a car passing down the road, there was the brief glimpse of a dark figure, walking steadily, quickly eastward. There was something in the way the figure moved. Calvin started the Explorer and pulled out.

He turned right onto Hawthorne Road and drove a block before his headlights caught the shadowy figure walking off to the side of the street. He pulled up alongside of him. It was Samuel. Calvin smiled, braked to walking speed, leaned over, and rolled down the passenger side window. "Are you sure you want to walk all the way to Saint Augustine?" he asked.

Startled, Samuel stopped short. Calvin hit his brakes. After a quick look at one another, Samuel turned his head and started walking again. "Stay away from me, Cal," he said over his shoulder.

Calvin came up along side of him again, keeping pace. "Why, Sam? Do you think you might want to shoot me too, like you wanted to shoot Godwin?"

Samuel only glared at Calvin while he continued walking.

"Hey, man," Calvin said. "if you want to kill somebody . . . could we at least talk about it first?"

"Go home, Calvin," Samuel said angrily, "you don't want to be a part of this."

"You're gonna get yourself killed, Sam."

"It wouldn't be the first time," Samuel said flatly, looking straight ahead.

Frustration written on his face, Calvin stopped the SUV. He watched his friend continue to walk ahead. "Damn it," he said to himself. Samuel was getting beyond his headlights. His hands tightened on the steering wheel. "The hell you are!" he yelled, his face contorting in anger. He jammed his foot down on the gas pedal. The rear wheels screeched as the Explorer shot forward.

Samuel heard the roar of the engine and turned, lifting a hand to see beyond the headlights. An instant flash of memory overwhelmed him—he saw and felt a car coming toward him, hitting him, and running him over. Now, again, he saw Calvin racing toward him. Frozen he waited for the impact but, at the last second, the vehicle veered off and passed him by.

Calvin cut in front of Samuel, braked hard to a skidding stop, and got out. He slammed the door in anger. "Whoa! Whoa! Whoa!" he said, walking toward Samuel. "You've really gone off the deep end, Sam!"

Samuel stopped and watched Calvin come toward him.

"This is really screwed up," Calvin said, "and if I hadn't told you about Timothy's book . . . I wouldn't be out here trying to stop you from messing up your life more than you already have." He stopped, face to face with Samuel, taking a stand, his eyes set in determination.

Surprised at Calvin's anger, Samuel felt a calm come over him. "Yeah, Cal," he said, "my life is messed up, but not because of you. Godwin's book only helped me remember the things I already knew. So, buddy, you're off the hook . . . you can go home. Please, man, you're my best friend. Please go home."

"Not so fast, Sam," Calvin said, holding up a hand. "Have you forgotten that you can tell what people are thinking? How do you know you didn't get it from me, before you read it?"

Samuel shook his head. "That's not the way it's been."

"Are you sure? . . . Are you reading me right now? . . . Because, Sam, I'm thinking you should be headed back on your way to the institute—so what if you know a book before you read it? Why would you want to kill the guy who wrote it?"

Samuel had never seen Calvin so adamant about anything. He took a deep breath. "Okay, Cal, fine. I'll tell you what you won't believe.

Calvin crossed his arms over his chest. "Try me," he said.

Samuel thumped himself in the chest with a thumb. "It's just like I told you. *I* was Captain Steven Darnell. My nightmares *are* the dreams of memories. My memories. Among those memories is the life of Victor Wilton."

"Whoa!" Calvin said, shaking his head and throwing his hands up in the air. "Come on, Sam. Wilton is a frigging fictional character." He started pacing and gesturing with his hands. "Why can't you get that through your head?"

Samuel looked at him levelly; he didn't know why anyone would ever believe him. "What's in my head is the memory of my wife and two daughters that were raped and slaughtered by Sebastian Loxton. That's what's in my head, Cal." Samuel knew that his words, or the way he'd said them, had gotten to his friend. If nothing else, he could tell he now understood that, at least, these things were real to him. "I've had that memory with me long before Godwin's book, and it was never shared with anyone. Only one other person could have known it happened."

"Oh," Calvin said, his voice full of sudden realization. "So, you went after Godwin, thinking he was Loxton . . . well, then why didn't you kill him?"

"I can see people for who they are, Cal, beyond what they appear to be." Samuel shook his head. "Timothy Godwin is not Sebastian Loxton."

Calvin put his hands out at his sides. "Well, I could have told you that."

Samuel frowned and cocked his head at Calvin.

"Well, let's go," Calvin said.

"Go where?"

"To find out if you're delusional or a paranoid schizophrenic . . . I strongly suspect both."

"Okay. So how do you plan to do that?"

"How else?" Calvin said. He turned around started back to the Explorer. "I'll take you where you want to go . . . as usual," he said over his shoulder.

Samuel stood on the dark roadside for a moment, watching Calvin walk away. The hint of a smile came to the corner of his mouth. He broke into a jog and followed.

They reached the SUV at the same time; Samuel opened the passenger door and stopped. "How did you know I'd be headed to Saint Augustine?"

Calvin looked at him. "It's in the book." They got in and closed the doors. "By the way," Calvin said, shifting into drive, "you owe me an autographed copy of *The Journeymen Diaries*." He looked back in his side mirror for oncoming traffic and pulled out onto the road. "But, I doubt Godwin's gonna be interested in signing anything any time soon."

CHAPTER TWELVE

STANLEY'S PUB WAS A QUIET LITTLE PLACE, just a couple of blocks from campus. The warm, soft lighting fit its rustic décor: brick walls and a wide-planked, oak floor.

"This is my kind of place," Nathan said, leading Timothy through the door. There was one older man sitting at the far end of the bar and a middle-aged couple sitting at a table in the corner. He swept his hand out to indicate the whole room. "An environment totally free of obnoxious undergraduates—a rare treat in this town. The Sinatra and jazz records on the juke box keep them at bay, kind of a pest control, if you will."

Timothy smiled as they walked up to the middle of the bar and sat down.

"Scotch, rocks," Nathan said to the barmaid, and looked to Timothy.

"Same," Timothy said. "But make mine a double, please."

Nathan looked at him with concern, but said nothing. He waited until after the barmaid set the drinks down, smiled, and turned away. "A double? Steady, old man," he said.

Timothy managed a weak, unconvincing smile, then removed his glasses and rubbed his face with his hands. He grabbed the double and took a big drink. "It was horrible, Nathan. He looked at me with sheer hatred in his eyes."

"I can only imagine," Nathan said. He paused and exhaled before going on. "You're not the first person to have been threatened for publishing a book. Fame has its price," he said in a conciliatory tone.

Timothy turned to him and snapped, "Well, I don't see you wearing a bulletproof vest." He took another swallow of the scotch.

"I'm a theologist, Timothy and I haven't written anything that could be regarded as heresy."

"Heresy?" Timothy said, his voice rising in incredulous surprise. *The Journeymen Diaries* isn't based on any religion."

Nathan held up a cautioning finger. "That you know of. Those manuscripts had to come from somewhere."

"I . . . uhhh . . . ," Timothy started and stopped himself. He stared at Nathan and looked away. Catching the barmaid looking at him he raised his glass.

She walked over smiling. "Another scotch?"

"Absolutely, please," Timothy said.

Nathan nodded her away. "No, I'm good," he said.

While bending and filling a glass with ice, the young woman stared at Timothy. "You're Timothy Godwin, aren't you?" she asked.

"Yes. Yes, I am," he said.

She put the fresh drink down in front of him and said, "I hate to do this, but would you sign my book?" Batting her eyes, she gave him a bright, pleading smile.

"Your fans are everywhere," Nathan said, looking at the barmaid, his voice dripping with sarcasm.

Timothy laughed and smiled at her. "Sure, I'd love to."

The woman stepped away and the anxiety came back into Timothy's face. He paused and started to turn toward Nathan twice before he finally spoke. "I don't know where the documents came from. My father left the house in the middle of the night and didn't come back." He shrugged. "Later . . . the police called and told us that he was hit and killed by a drunk driver while helping someone—an old woman, with a flat tire." He gave Nathan a grim, bitter smile. "He had the manuscripts with him when he died. It's my guess that he was going to use them to finish his book." Turning, he looked and paused before he said, "*The Journeymen Diaries.*"

Nathan's eyebrows went up and his lips fell open in surprise.

"So," Timothy went on, looking at their reflections in the mirror behind the bar. "Now you know. The story was my dad's idea, not mine. I found a ledger he had been writing in for years. It was mostly random thoughts and fragmented stories," He shrugged. "I just took what he'd written and pieced it all together. I never anticipated the success it would have. And, God, having to write a sequel . . ."

Nathan interrupted him, laying a hand on the sleeve of Timothy's sport coat. "So, you didn't write the book based on the manuscript?"

"No," Timothy said. "But, apparently he did. A lot of what was written in his ledger is very similar to what Tasha has translated. What you've seen is just a fraction of what there is. I have old hand-written pages in English, French, German . . . it goes on, along with old photos of people dating back as far as the late eighteen-hundreds."

"Ancestors?" Nathan asked. He was looking at Timothy in rapt attention.

Timothy shook his head. "Not within my lineage, nothing seems to fit with my family history."

The barmaid returned proudly bearing her book and a fresh drink. "This one's on me," she said, setting down the glass and handing the book to Timothy.

"Thank you," Timothy said. He patted his coat pocket for a pen and started to look around the bar top. "Errr . . ."

Nathan rolled his eyes and handed him a pen.

"Who should I make this out to?'

"Stacy," the woman said.

Timothy signed the book and handed it back to her with a smile.

"Thank you," Stacy said.

"The pleasure's mine."

Nathan rolled his eyes again and exhaled in exasperated impatience. Stacy walked away hugging her book to her breast. "So . . . , they weren't ancestors?" he asked.

Timothy looked at him a moment then shook his head. "No, I researched all of the names I could find in the manuscripts . . ."

"And, what did you find?"

"I found out," Timothy said with a look of shame on his face, "each and every one of them had been murdered or committed suicide . . . at least those that had any history I could find."

"So . . . ," Nathan said, "now . . . you're thinking that your father was . . . murdered?"

Timothy's eyes went wide. "Wouldn't you! Especially after tonight?"

"You think there's a connection between the kid and the manuscript?"

Timothy was slow to respond, his face lost in thought. "I remember something," he said. "Something Tasha told me the other night. She was reading . . . translating . . . from the Sumerian text. Reading aloud, she said, 'the end is near, a time for a new beginning.'" He looked at Nathan. "That's what the kid said, just before he lowered the gun—just when I was sure he was going to blow my head off. He said, 'Time for a new beginning.' So, to answer your question, Nathan, is there a connection? I'm pretty, damn sure there is. I don't know what it is, but I can tell you it scares the hell out of me."

CALVIN PARKED THE EXPLORER in the empty beach parking lot and turned off the headlights. The sign read, "National Park Service, U. S Department of Interior, Castillo De San Marcos National Monument." It was the first time he'd actually seen the ancient Spanish fortress in Saint Augustine. At a quarter past twelve in the morning, lit by the full moon, it was a hulking, eerie sight. Massive, stone walls ran down from the parking lot all the way to the shoreline and on, into the surf. Atop the walls, watchtowers stood against the moonlit sky like squat, dark, evil sentries.

"Oh my God!" Calvin said. "It's just like in the book. "But in the book, it's called Fort Saint Mark."

Samuel stared at the fortress, a knowing far off look in his eyes. "It was called Fort Saint Mark, in 1782."

"This is creepy. This whole *thing* is creepy. Why can't you have nightmares about amusement parks or Vegas?"

"Well, it doesn't look like it's changed much in two-hundred years," Samuel said. He turned and looked at Calvin. "But this isn't where we need to be."

Calvin looked confused. "Isn't this where you wanted to go? In the book . . ."

"No, not here," Samuel said, shaking his head. "Drive around. I'll tell you where to turn."

"What is it?" Calvin asked.

"I don't know, but I'll know it when I see it."

"Oh, wonderful," Calvin said under his breath, "here we go again." He started the SUV and pulled back out on the road. With Samuel directing they drove for several blocks through the old,

Spanish colonial part of town and out just past where the street lights ended.

Seeing the centuries old landmarks, Samuel was struck by a sense of déjà vu. He felt confident his instincts would guide him to where he needed to go. Moving slowly down a darkened street, it abruptly hit him.

"Here," Samuel said, "pull over here."

Calvin slammed on the brakes. He gave Samuel a quick look of surprise and lowered his head to look out through Samuel's window. The moonlight illuminated an old cemetery. It was fenced off with iron bars and stone columns. "Oh, are you freakin' kidding me?!" Calvin said. "Jeez, why does it always have to be a cemetery, Sam?"

Samuel was looking out the window. "Can you think of a better place that someone could count on being around a hundred years from now?"

"So, are you buried here too?"

"No," Samuel said, "just my past is buried here."

"Sam, ya' know—I don't have any memories of any past lives."

"Lucky you. I wish I didn't."

They got out of the Explorer. The hot, humid, sea air surrounded them, sticking to their skin like a wet blanket. Samuel dug in the back of the SUV and pulled out the flashlights.

"What about the shovels?" Calvin asked.

Samuel shook his head. "We're not going to need them."

"Well, that's a relief. We don't have to dig you up again."

After boosting Calvin over the six-foot iron spike fence, Samuel climbed over himself. They walked up the cemetery's main drive into its interior. Samuel's eyes were fixed on a group of white marble mausoleums and large monuments that glowed in the moonlight.

CHAPTER THIRTEEN

A DESCENDING FOG played eerily with the beam of the flashlight as tombstones were illuminated and shadowed.

"Jesus, Sam," Calvin said quietly, "this place is creepier than the last one." He went on talking, prattling nervously, while he looked around and hurried to stay close to Samuel. "Boy, that's rich, this is the *second* time I'm robbing a freaking grave. So, you *are* telling me there's *no* corpse this time . . . right?"

"Not that I can remember."

"That's not making me feel any better. What are we looking for then?"

Samuel stopped in front of a mausoleum. The word "Alexandria" was carved in the stone above the door.

"Whoa," Calvin chuckled uneasily, "Alexandria. Like in Egypt . . . the old library?"

"Yeah. The name seemed appropriate, at the time I built it."

"*You* built this?"

"Yeah."

"So, how do we get in?" Calvin asked, looking at its iron door. You still remember how to do that?"

Samuels eyes swept around the door and the face of the stone. His eyes settled on the cross shaped hole that was cut into the stone just above the name. Something, an instinct, made him abruptly walk to the back of burial chamber. Calvin followed, close on his heels. At the back wall of the vault, Samuel saw an iron cross inlaid into the stone. He reached out and brushed a hand across the three protruding, decorative stones that were spaced evenly across the back wall. They were warm and clammy in the Florida night air. For no reason beyond an impulse, he pushed hard on the end stone. It moved inward. As it did, the iron cross moved out, extending inches from its stone encasement. Samuel put his fingers around it. He pulled on the cross and it slid out, free from the wall. Holding it in his hand he examined it in the flashlight beam. It was an iron rod, six inches long, with identical crosses on each end.

"What is that?" Calvin asked.

Samuel looked at him, then walked back to the front of the mausoleum. "It's a key," he said, as they approached the door. He reached and slid an end into the cross shaped recess. It was an exact fit. He turned it, straining hard against the ancient, corroded mechanism. There was a hollow clank and the iron door gave a spine chilling creak as it opened a few inches.

"Whoa, holy crap, will you look at that!" Calvin whispered, in amazement. "I guess you *have* done this before."

Samuel gave him a brief smile. "What was it that you said? I was delusional or maybe a paranoid schizophrenic—if not both. Right?" He placed his hand on the door and pushed it open. From the stone black of the interior, the sobering odor of the ancient world came to his nostrils.

"Okay, you've made your point," said Calvin, as he watched Samuel step inside the mausoleum. He hesitated a moment, looked behind him. The misty fog was beginning to thicken, hovering just over the gravestones. He ducked and hurried in behind Samuel.

They scanned the interior with their flashlights. There were marble busts among an assortment of old weapons: swords, daggers, and a battle axe, metal vases, and plates of silver, bronze, and gold. Several ornate flags were leaning against the wall. On a stone bench that ran around the perimeter there were strong boxes and crates. The floor was littered with gold and silver coins, Spanish doubloons, artifacts and jewelry. Hundreds of loose precious stones shimmered in the beam of their lights. Propped up in the corner was an Egyptian death mask.

"Forget Vegas. I can't believe all this!" Calvin said in wonder. "This has got to be worth millions."

"Yeah," Samuel said. "But there's a downside—a big one. For me to be right about all this . . . means that you can count on Loxton being out there somewhere too."

"Well, okay," Calvin said. "But I don't get it. If he's not Timothy, how the heck could he know so much to write the book?"

"That's what I'm here to figure out." Samuel's light beam found an ancient, ironwood chest. "The answer lies in there," he said. He stepped over to the chest and raised the top. It was empty. He felt a wave of anguish hit him with a physical jolt, as a vision, a series of memories, came hurtling at him in rapid succession.

FRANK LEWIS AWAKENED gasping in terror. His eyes, wide in panic, scanned the dark for the man who was trying to kill him. He whimpered aloud; it couldn't have been only a dream. Laying his head back down on the pillow, he tried to calm himself. Furtively, his eyes shot to the dark silhouette of his wife on the other side of the bed. The last thing he wanted to do was to awaken Karen. He'd put her through enough. His heart pounded in his ears, a booming, slow cadence—boom . . . boom . . . boom. Surely, he thought, she would hear it and wake up. As he slowly sat up and eased out of bed, he realized his pajamas and the bed sheets were soaked in sweat. Walking very softly, he padded into the bathroom and closed the door.

Reaching up for the medicine cabinet door, he was caught unaware by his own reflection in the mirror. Two years ago he'd been a healthy, happy, and young forty-three. Now, his kind, pleasant eyes were bloodshot, surrounded by black circles, and sunken into the emaciated face of a broken man. "Jesus, I'm a basket case," he thought.

He yanked open the medicine cabinet to get away from his own image. The sickening feeling was starting again, the deadening certainty that there was something very wrong with him and it wasn't going to go away. His trembling hand went to the dozen neatly arranged pill bottles on the bottom shelf. Something had to help—give him some meager bit of comfort. Fumbling from one to another, squinting to read the names of the medications, he picked up one to bring it closer to his face and dropped it. Both hands wildly swung after it and he was able to snag it before it hit the floor. Clutching the bottle to his stomach, he looked in panic toward the bathroom door and listened. Please God, she didn't need to know. He didn't hear anything and brought the pill bottle away from his face so he could read it without his glasses. Yes, that was the one, the tranquilizer the doctor had said would help to calm him. He took several deep breaths to steady his hands and started twisting at the lid.

"Got to take the medication," he mumbled aloud, trying to reassure himself, "got to give the medication a chance." That's what they kept telling him, the doctors and Karen; the medication and therapy would work, but he had to work with them. "Damn, childproof lids!" he cursed under his breath.

Suddenly, high in his nostril, came the humid, fresh, scent of sea air, the danger, the death—his death!—came back, overwhelming him. His legs gave way at the violent force of the memory and he was thrown to the wall, he slid down to a sitting position on the floor. Angrily, he threw the pill bottle, clattering against the far wall.

"It's not in my head!" he hissed furiously through gritted teeth.

There was a soft knock on the door. "Frank?"

His head bolted upright. "It's okay, honey . . . , I'm okay."

"I heard a bang," Karen said.

The caring sweetness of her voice tore at Frank's heart. He'd—this damned thing—had put her through so much. He forced a laugh. "Just my fumble fingered self, dropped a pill bottle. You go back to sleep, honey."

"Are you coming back soon?"

"Yeah," he said quickly. "Yes, in a little bit."

He held his breath while he waited for her to settle back into bed, then he put his face in his hands and fought back his tears. What was it? What was tormenting him? First, when Karen finally insisted that he see a psychiatrist, they said it was stress that caused the debilitating nightmares. He hadn't told Karen, but he was scared to death and, in truth, he was glad to see the doctors. If taking a pill would stop the terror, he was all for it.

No, he'd told them, told them all, it wasn't just dreams. It was stark, vivid reality. They all gave him their calm, knowing nods of understanding. "Frank, that's the way of having vivid, chronic nightmares," they'd insisted. "They are real in every sense of *your* reality, mentally and emotionally they *are* real. You know that, Frank. You practiced clinical psychology for twenty years, how did you respond to patients with similar parasomnia disorders?"

They were so sure, so knowing, so certain, but they were wrong. His clinical experience was exactly what told him the dreams weren't caused by psychoses. Still, he'd tried to believe them for two years of counseling, meditation, and the pills—an endless series of pills. And where had it all left him? It not only shattered his career, it was destroying his life, one piece at a time.

The best wife any man could want was almost at the point of a breakdown over it. And his son, Tim, he was a great kid, always putting on a smile and saying he was okay. But Frank knew that, inside, the boy was devastated at seeing his father become a fearful wreck of a man.

In the dreams the horrible violence came fully alive. But even when he was awake the nagging prodding of . . . something . . . was there all of the time, always on him. There wasn't much he was sure of anymore, but he was sure that there was something—some force—that was driving him to know more. In his heart, he knew it with certainty. And, he knew the nightmares wouldn't stop with all the pills and therapies in the world. It wouldn't stop until he understood what he needed to know. And, in his heart, he knew there was something he had to do. He had to find out what it was.

Frank reached over, picked up the pill bottle, got to his feet, and placed it back in the cabinet. He turned out the light and quietly opened the door. Tiptoeing, he walked out of the bedroom and down the hallway to his study. Reaching up to the shelf above his desk, he pulled down the bound log book and set it down. He sat and opened it, flipping through the hundreds of pages of notes he'd made over the last two years in his small neat script. At the first open space, he wrote, "August 10th, 1992."

As always, he was meticulous in recording every detail of the dream, stopping every now and then to make himself remember every facet he possibly could. The fort was there; the ancient military installation that he'd seen in dreams again and again. He was describing it once more when something stopped him. Closing his eyes he tried to see the scene. A vision of the front of the fort came to him. The ominous stone walls, thirty feet thick, the parapets hulking above . . . but . . . what was it? He made himself start again, focusing on the entrance, the arched portal to . . . a sallyport, where a man went through one door and then it was closed before a second one was opened.

"Damn it," he said aloud, "what?"

Then it came to him, a crest over the arched entry! "Fort Saint Mark!"

He swiveled in his chair to the computer set up on the small side desk and started it up. "Come on, come on," he said, his fingers poised above the keyboard, "boot up, for Christ's sake." Was there a Fort Saint Mark or was it just the fabrication of an insane mind? He was pretty sure he'd never heard of a fort by that name. Why would he make that up? Finally, the small screen came to light. Technically, he was on administrative leave from the clinic at the university and still had full access to their intranet. He put in his password to enter the university's search engine. He typed, "Fort St. Mark," and, suddenly fearful, sat back in the chair. Did he really want to know?

In spite of his fear, his hand shot out like it had a mind of its own and slapped the enter button. He tried to ready himself with all that was left of his shattered life and mind. After what seemed like forever, a page came up. He leaned in squinting, his finger on the screen, he went down the long list. Quickly he dismissed several articles that were about something to do with St. Mark but had nothing to do with a fort. Then, there it was, in the middle of the page, "Fort St. Mark." He made himself read the name again. It was a historical paper written by a professor at the university, titled "The British Occupation of Florida." He clicked on it. Looking for St. Mark in the text, his finger scanned rapidly, on the second page there it was. It was in St. Augustine! The old Spanish fort, the Castillo de San Marcos, was "occupied by the British army from 1763 to 1784," and, during that period, renamed the fortress "Fort St. Mark." Scrolling down he found an underlined link to "photos." He clicked it and there it was, staring him in the face, the fort that had been the setting for so many, tormenting nightmares. His mouth agape, his lower jaw began to quiver. He slowly stood up. Tears rolled down Frank Lewis's face. Careful not to wake Karen, he grabbed some clothes from the bedroom, dressed, and went out to the garage.

Racing through the black, moonless night he was able to get to the beachfront parking lot for the Castillo De San Marcos in just over an hour. He got out of the car and walked across the grass like a zombie, his eyes fixed on the old fort. Only the outline of the monstrous, squatting structure was visible in the security lights. This had to be it. He could hear the waves breaking on the beach and smell the warm, sea air; it was just like in the dream. It was real.

Suddenly, he stopped. Was *this* all just a dream or reality? Surely he would die here again. Were they waiting for him? Was that what the dreams were telling him? Was it all just to lure him to another horrible death—a real death? He started backing slowly away for a few steps before he began to run back to his car.

He didn't know what to do. Surely, he thought, Karen would have missed him by now and would be frantic. He knew he should head back, but he'd finally found something that connected his torment to reality and he knew in his bones there was more. There was more and it was *here*!

Driving aimlessly down the beach highway, his eyes searched the darkened tourist shops and restaurants for clues to where he needed to go. They meant nothing to him, but there was something in the smell and feel of the soft air that drove him on. For no reason, he turned down a narrow side street. It looked like more junk souvenir shops.

He had all but passed a small, darkened structure on his right before he slammed on the brakes. There was a sign. It was the old St. Augustine schoolhouse. He stared at it through the open window of his car. There was an eerie sense that he'd been there, some fragment of a buried memory. It wasn't anything he remembered from the nightmares. He tried to force his mind to remember. Horror crawled up his spine. His mind found an instant glimpse of the bloody bodies of murdered children—two girls. A crushing sense of loss washed over him. It was too much! He sped away, screeching the tires on the deserted street.

At the end of the street he turned to the left. The commercial places seemed to be thinning into an older, residential area. Ahead, the headlights picked up a sign, he leaned forward to try and read it as he approached. "The Saint Augustine Cemetery," it said. There was an arrow pointing down a side street on the right. He stopped in the middle of the road and stared at the sign for a moment, then, like a light being turned on, he was struck by a sense of clarity. Something in him seemed to take over his will. Afraid, but compelled to follow his instincts, he turned right.

Within a short time, Frank was running through the cemetery, breathing heavily. The urgency of fear relentlessly driving him, he franticly searched, his flashlight giving him brief glimpses of the tombstones, monuments, and mausoleums. Moving faster, the beam swung wildly up into the moss laden, ancient trees, then down to the ground at his feet. He stumbled, almost falling in his haste.

"Damn it!" he cursed himself in a hushed voice.

Frank moved forward again, searching. His light caught a mausoleum made of white stone then moved away. He suddenly stopped and brought the beam back to the structure. Starting forward again, his pace slowed to deliberate, cautious steps, moving directly toward the rusted, iron door illuminated by the now unwavering light. The sweat rolled down his face, his shirt was soaked and clinging against his chest. The heavy thud of his pounding heart made the front of the shirt move with a visible jerk. Frank's eyes moved up to see the name cut into the stone above the door. "Alexandria," it read.

His jaw dropped, his mouth opening wide in shock. "Oh God!" he said. "It's real. It's really here."

CHAPTER FOURTEEN

SAMUEL KNEW NOW THAT IT WAS REAL; it was all real! He had been there—grabbing hands reaching down, emptying the ironwood chest, putting the contents into a leather bag, Frank's hands—*his* hands. He could see it all, the bag lying beside him on the front seat of the car speeding through the night. Then there were blinding headlights and the sickening physical pain. Samuel jolted under the crushing force of the vision as his very being was struck by the oncoming vehicle. Through the fog of his trance, he began to hear Calvin's voice.

"Sam, Sam," Calvin called. "Are you okay?" He had come forward and had his hands on Samuel's shoulders, supporting him.

Samuel blinked. "Yeah . . . , yeah," he said, staggering, then straightening up. "Yeah . . . , thanks, man."

"What was that?" Calvin asked. "You jerked like you grabbed an electric fence or something."

"I'm okay," Samuel told him.

"It's empty," Calvin said as looked into the chest. "Why would it be empty?"

Still feeling a bit woozy, Samuel closed eyes and said, "Because, I've already been here, Cal."

"What? When?"

Suddenly, Samuel felt a sense of danger deep in his stomach. Something was wrong. Life came back into his eyes and he turned to Calvin. "I think we need to go. We need to go now," he said, the urgency of fear in his voice.

Samuel wasted no time. Nearer to the door, he was the first one out. As soon as Calvin was out he closed and locked the door. "I'll be right back," he said and raced around to the rear and set the cross-like key back into its resting place in the stone.

Calvin was squinting into the darkness. "Please, man, hurry," he pled.

When Samuel returned to the front he immediately stopped short in alarm at the terror he saw in his friend's eyes.

"Saa-am," Calvin said, "who the hell are *those* guys?"

Samuel looked and saw three shadowy, hooded figures, standing, waiting amongst the gravestones. Masked, dressed in black body armor and cloaks, they stood like phantoms of death. They had weapons at the ready; medieval weapons, flails and maces. "Oh God. No," Samuel uttered in a low voice.

Suddenly, Samuel threw an arm around Calvin's neck, placing him in a chokehold. He could feel Calvin's body quaking in terror. Pulling the pistol from his pocket, he put the muzzle against the side of Calvin's head. "Do exactly what I tell you, Cal," he said.

"Wha . . . what—," Calvin stuttered.

"Move!" Samuel hissed at him as he pushed him forward. The menacing figures began to come towards them. Samuel jerked the gun away from Calvin's head and pointed it directly at the nearest man. They kept coming. With a night shattering blast of light and sound the gun fired. The bullet crashed into the face of his target, dropping him instantly to the ground.

Samuels' senses were aflame, aware of movement behind him; he whirled around to see two more of them. They were too close—there before he could even aim the pistol. One of them swung a flail that wrapped around his arm. The phantom pulled, dragging Samuel toward him. At the same moment, another attacker grabbed Calvin. With a violent kick, Samuel knocked his assailant away, and shot him square in the chest. The flail still wrapped around his arm, he turned back around to see Calvin being dragged away. He aimed and fired again.

At the blast the attacker went limp and both he and Calvin went to the ground. In furious panic, Calvin kicked and shoved the man off of him, and scrambled to his feet. "Get away from me!" he screamed in a high-pitched voice Samuel had never heard before.

"Run!" Samuel yelled at him.

Calvin wasted no time flying off through the dark towards the gate. The two remaining attackers, squared off with Samuel. He raised the revolver, aimed, and pulled the trigger. There was only a click that seemed to him as loud as a rifle shot. He pulled the trigger again only to hear another click. The sound sent the masked attackers running at him at a full speed. In reflex he threw the gun at one of them. He unwrapped the flail twisted around his arm. The first attacker closed in. With his mace drawn back, he swung. Samuel waited an instant before he ducked under the whistling, heavy, spiked ball. In the same fluid movement he came up with the flail. It caught the jaw of the attacker, ripping off his mask. The man screamed, staggered off, and fell to the ground. Suddenly, Samuel felt a crashing blow to his head. He cried out in agony and fell to his knees. In his mind there was an awareness of the man getting ready to hit him again. Desperately, he told his limbs to move, to fight, but he was helpless. The second blow hit him in the chest so hard that he felt his whole body move. He keeled over, face first into the dirt.

The dark figure stood over Samuel. He reached inside of his cloak and pulled out a pair of iron wrist shackles. Just as he picked up one of Samuel's limp hands, there was the roar of an engine and the screech of tires from out on the road. The assailant looked up. The Explorer lurched forward and, with a screeching bang, rammed through the cemetery gate. The man dropped

Samuel's hand and straightened up. Squinting against the headlights he watched it come up the drive moving faster and faster. He widened his stance in readiness and made a half-step back in apprehension. At the speed the SUV was moving there was nowhere for it to go without crashing into something.

Calvin had the gas pedal to the floor; his face was a mask of fierce, angry determination. "Hang on, Sam!" he yelled. Staying on the drive, he built up more and more speed. He was closing fast on his target. "Holy crap, I hope this works!" he screamed.

At the last second, almost coming even with the cloaked figure, the Explorer suddenly veered off the road. Sparks flew as it banged loudly into one headstone then careened wildly into another. The beams of the headlights bouncing in an insane, bizarre lightshow bracketed the target. The man froze for a moment then took several uncertain steps back, as though he was unsure as to which way to go. Finally, too late, he broke into a run to his left. In a few steps, he screamed as the SUV caught him with its left front fender.

The sickening thud and the bounce of the tire as it passed over the man brought a vicious, victorious smile to Calvin's face. "Take that, asshole!" he yelled. He braked, shifted into park, swung the door open, and jumped out. "Sam!" he yelled, running to his friend.

Samuel was just starting to come to and had managed to push himself into a half sitting position when Calvin got to him.

"You okay?" Calvin said, bending and helping him to his feet. "Come on! Let's get the hell outta here."

Sluggish, Samuel got to his feet. He felt a throbbing, sharp pain on the back of his head and his chest hurt when he tried to breathe. "I'm okay, Cal," he managed to mumble, he pushed his friend's arms off of him and started to walk away.

Calvin's eyes widened in terror. He could hear one of the attackers moaning in agony right behind him. "Where are you going, Sam! Come on, man! Let's go!"

Staggering a little, Samuel was searching for something on the ground in the reflected light from the headlights.

"What are you doing?" Calvin asked, in an incredulous, exasperated tone.

Samuel stopped, bent over, and swiped the pistol off the ground. He turned around and looked at Calvin. "He'll know where he is," he said pointing the gun at one of the wounded attackers. "He'll know." He walked over to the man and grabbed him by the cloak, lifting him off the ground. It was the man he'd unmasked with the flail. Staring into the frightened eyes, Samuel felt nothing but cold anger. He was looking down into the face of a mere mortal. The man gasped, his hand to his throat, desperately trying to stem the flow of spurting blood.

"Wo ist der Fleischgeworden?" he asked, hissing into the dying man's face. "Where is the . . ." The man's body quaked convulsively, then stilled, and went limp. Samuel let go of the cloak, letting the body fall to the ground, and stepped back. He turned to Calvin who'd come up beside him, he saw his friend's face looking down and contorted in horror.

"Let's go," Samuel said.

"Yeah," Calvin said. For a moment he was still frozen, looking at the maimed corpse, then he broke into a panicked dash back to the truck, tripping and almost falling along the way.

In Calvin's haste, he backed the Explorer, sideswiping several tombstones before he reached the drive. He sped to the gate and, with a screech of tires, made a hard, sliding turn onto the roadway. They did not see the cloaked figure that stepped out of the dark and into the road, his eyes fixed on the rear license plate.

Samuel was breathing hard and wincing with pain. He held a hand to his chest.

"You okay, Sam?" Calvin asked.

"It . . . hurts when I . . . a bit . . . when I breathe . . . I'll be fine." Samuel said. He looked at Calvin, his face illuminated by the dashboard lights. His head swiveled back and forth, from the road, to Samuel, and then back again. Samuel could see Calvin's fear, concern, and relief. Slowly, a smile came to Samuel's face.

"What's so damn funny?" Calvin asked. "Do you have any idea how close we came to getting killed back there?"

Samuel laid a hand on Calvin's shoulder, shook him gently, and started to laugh. "Yeah, I do, and you still came back for me. Thanks. You should'a seen yourself charging in through that place. I didn't know you had it in you, Cal." Samuel's face grew serious. "That's more than anyone's ever done for me."

Calvin's gave him a shy smile and his face turned red with embarrassment. He shrugged and, blinking, turned his eyes back to the road. "That's what friends do. Besides, I couldn't just leave you . . . and all the excitement behind."

Samuel picked up the pistol and flipped open the cylinder and chuckled, "I never thought to check it." Three chambers of the revolver were empty; he pushed the ejector rod and removed the spent shells. "Sorry for holding the gun to your head."

"Yeah!" Calvin said. "What the heck was that about?"

"I needed you to stay put until I could figure out what was going on."

"Jeez, you scared the crap out of me. Who *were* those guys?"

"Anhangers," Samuel answered, clicking the cylinder back in place, "followers of the Fleischgeworden . . . the Incarnate. They exist only to serve him."

"*The Journeymen Diaries*?" Calvin looked at him in disbelief. "Is everything in the book true?"

Samuel shrugged. "Yeah . . . , for the most part."

"So, what did the anhangers want?"

"Me. Alive," Samuel answered. "Luckily for you . . . they didn't know which one of us to take."

For a few minutes, Calvin drove in silence before he asked, "Okay, so, why would they want you alive . . . when Loxton keeps killing you?"

Samuel shook his head. "That's got me wondering too. I don't know—but it can't be good."

"I can't believe this," Calvin said excitedly, "it's like we're actually living Timothy's book." He looked down nervously at the gun in Samuel's hand. "Nice shooting earlier. Were you Butch Cassidy or somethin' in another life?"

"Annie Oakley, I think," Samuel said with a laugh, "but I'm not sure."

"I can't picture you in a dress with a rifle."

"Well, that makes two of us."

An hour into the long drive back to Gainesville, Samuel started to feel better. He sat back and tried to think. Calvin had a good question: why didn't they just kill him when they had him helpless on the ground? There was something going on that he'd never had nightmares about and hadn't read in Timothy's book. He didn't like it.

When Calvin finally pulled into his parking space at the duplex, it was the middle of the night. He stretched and yawned. "Ya' know, Sam," he said, "it's amazing how friggin' tired you can get kickin' anhangers ass."

Samuel looked at him, knowing his friend couldn't know the full danger of the situation. He got out and walked quickly around the SUV and opened the driver's side door.

Calvin looked at him in surprise. "What's this, valet parking?"

"I have to take it from here, Cal," Samuel said, giving him a serious look. "I need the Explorer."

"Oh, no," Calvin said, shaking his head. "You don't even know how to drive. Besides, we're a team."

Samuel nodded his head. "Yeah, Cal, we're a team, a great team, but you've done all you can do. You can't be a part of this anymore. They would have killed you, back there. Dying is only another beginning for me. I don't know if it's that way for you or anyone else . . . other than him." He motioned with his head for Calvin to get out of the SUV.

Calvin hesitated a second before slowly getting out. He moved aside and stood like a dejected little boy, while Samuel got in behind the wheel.

"Are you sure you know how to drive?" Calvin asked.

"I did in 1945."

"Oh, that's comforting," Calvin said and they both laughed, before Calvin stopped, his smile gone.

"Give me three days," Samuel said. "If I don't come back . . . tell the police I stole your car. That will get you off the hook with all this."

Calvin lowered his eyes for a second then looked up at his friend with watery eyes. "You're not coming back . . . are you?"

Samuel blinked and hesitated before he answered. "Probably not in this life, Cal."

They both managed grim, supportive smiles. Samuel backed out and left Calvin standing there watching him drive off.

Calvin turned to his apartment and went inside. After taking a shower, he sat on the living room couch, eating some leftover Chinese food while he watched an old Star Trek rerun. His face lost in thought, he jumped at a sharp knock on his door. It was the middle of the night. He stood and walked across his living room to the front window. There was a large, black sedan in his parking space. He opened the door to see two men holding gold badges in his face. Both of them were in plain clothes.

"Y . . . yes," he stuttered in shocked surprise.

"Calvin Adkins?" one of them asked. "Police. Do you mind if we come in and have a word with you?"

"Ahh . . . , sure," Calvin said, "sure." He'd held the door open for them. "What's it all about, officers?" The two came in and Calvin closed the door. "You two wouldn't happen to be twins, would you?" They didn't return Calvin's smile. "It's just both of you, having . . . blond hair and blue eyes." Calvin's smile faded. "Ah . . . , forget it," he said. He moved to the couch and started to clear off a pile of books. "Sorry, for the mess. I wasn't expecting . . ." When he turned back around there was a Tazer pistol pointed at his chest. His face contorted in surprise. Before he could find words the Tazer fired with a loud "pop." The two probes sank into his chest and his twitching body collapsed to the floor.

The men moved forward and pulled a black hood over Calvin's head, and hand cuffed his arms behind his back. Before Calvin could fully recover from the paralyzing shock to his body, they quickly lifted him off the ground, carried him outside, and threw him into the backseat of a black sedan.

CHAPTER FIFTEEN

SAMUEL SLOWED THE EXPLORER as he turned into the late-night quiet of a subdivision. He leaned his head to one side and squinted to read the street signs.

"Forty-fourth Terrace," he said to himself, "that's it."

He drove even slower, looking from one side of the street to the other, trying to find a readable house number in the dim, shadowy illumination of the porch lights. The last thing he wanted was to draw attention by going around the block several times in the middle of the night. Then, to his right, there it was—twenty-three, ten—the home of Timothy Godwin.

"Okay, okay," he said as his eyes hungrily scanned, trying to see every detail in one pass. There was no car in the drive and the garage door was closed. While the living room window was illuminated with a low, soft light, the blinds were shuttered. Samuel grimaced in disappointment, there was no way he could be sure if anyone was home or not. His grip on the steering wheel tightened. "What now?" he wondered. He didn't like the idea of parking on the street where a strange, battered, old SUV was likely to be noticed.

With nothing coming to mind, he continued driving the three blocks to the end of the street. He pulled up at the stop sign;

his headlights illuminated an undeveloped, wooded area. Turning right, he drove along the edge of the dark woods until he saw a narrow, dirt road, little more than a trail, that ran into the area.

"That'll do," he said aloud.

He pulled into the woods until he was sure he was out of sight of the road, turned out his lights, and parked. Moving as quietly as possible, he got out of the Explorer and walked back towards the paved road. Close to the road, he stepped off into the woods and made his way back to the end of Timothy's street.

There was very little light filtering from the nearby homes to help Samuel make his way. Brambles and barbed vines grabbed at his feet while branches scratched at his face. He forced his legs through while he pushed the branches away as best he could. Struggling, he was surprised to find tears coming to his eyes. In a lifetime of feeling alone, Samuel had never felt so alone. Here he was, close—closer than he'd ever been—to finding some relief from the nightmare that had stalked him his whole life. But, hanging over the tantalizing promise of relief, was a growing, overwhelming sense of looming horror. Finally, reaching a point where he had a clear view down Godwin's street, he stopped. Exhausted, he sat down on the carpet of dead leaves. "All the endless questions," he thought, "and now maybe some answers." He blinked away the tears. "I've got to be right about this," he thought, "I can't be wrong again."

He sat and watched the seemingly endless stillness of the street. With his fatigue and the fear he was trying to ignore, his doubt began to magnify itself. Could he be wrong again? Was that the way it was supposed to be: maybe he was just born to spend his whole life in a maddening, never ending, cat-and-mouse game. And, right now, was he wrong to think the element of surprise gave him the upper hand?

TIMOTHY AND NATHAN came out of the front door of Stanley's bar and walked into its almost empty parking lot. "A detective, Jenkins, I think his name is, wants me to meet with him at the police station tomorrow morning," Timothy said squinting and turning his watch to the streetlight on the corner. "Later this morning, I should say."

"You going to be able to drive okay?" Nathan asked, with concern, as they stepped up to Timothy's car.

Timothy smiled. "Yeah, I'm okay." He turned and looked around the lot—a lone car drove by, heading down the deserted street.

"Patricia and I have an extra room, if you want to use it," Nathan said.

Timothy turned back to him and, for a second, looked confused. "Oh . . . , why, because of that kid?"

"You might feel safer, staying with us."

After hesitating for a moment, Timothy shook his head. He turned, unlocked, and opened his car door. "I appreciate it, Nathan, but if the kid was going to kill me he would have." He shrugged. "Besides, he doesn't know where I live. I'll be fine," He reached out and shook Nathan's hand. "But, thanks for the offer. You have a good night. And, hey, I appreciate your understanding."

Nathan waved his comment away. "It's only what you deserve," he said. "I made a rash judgment. Now, drive carefully and get some sleep." He smiled and walked to his car. Both men got in their cars and drove away.

CALVIN'S BODY QUIVERED WITH SHEER TERROR, with the black hood over his head, there was nothing but darkness, pain, and fear. He was suspended by wrist shackles with chains that were bolted to the ceiling of a stone walled room. With his toes barely able to brush against the floor, he moaned from the agony of his raw and bleeding wrists.

"Oh God," he mumbled to himself with tear filled eyes. Wheezing, he was almost ready to pass out from the pain when there was the noise of a door opening.

"P . . . p . . . please. . . ," Calvin whimpered at the sound. "What . . . what do you want?"

The hood was pulled off Calvin's head. His swollen, squinting eyes tried to adjust to the light. Someone stood before him wearing a gold, skeletal, death mask under a dark, hooded cloak. Around the menacing figure's neck, hung a gold, black sun medallion.

The Fleischgeworden looked directly into Calvin's eyes.

AT THE EDGE OF THE WOODS, across from Timothy's street, weak from exhaustion and pain, Samuel sat on the ground, struggling to keep his eyes open. His eyes closed and his head started to sink, when he jerked himself awake to see a car's headlights turn onto the far end of the street. It was coming up the street towards him. Fixated, he watched it slow down and pull into Timothy Godwin's driveway. In the quiet of night, he could hear the rumble of the garage door opening.

"Looks like you had a late night too, Tim," Samuel said, aloud. Waiting, he heard the garage door close. He stepped out of the woods and started walking up the street.

The next morning, the grinding clank of Timothy's garage door opening crashed into Samuel's deep sleep. He turned over with a groan and put his hand on his chest, there was still pain from the fight with the anhangers. His eyes widened as he realized that he was lying on the ground between a hedge and Timothy's house. It was daylight. He'd overslept. He ignored his pain and jumped into a crouching position. Keeping low to the ground he moved quickly to the corner of the house. He knew that his timing was crucial. He waited until he heard the sound of Timothy's car door opening and closing before he moved. Hunched over, he scooted to the wall beside the open garage door and took a quick peek inside. Samuel stayed low, trying to stay where he gauged the blind spot in the car's mirror to be. Down on his hands and knees, he moved along slowly up against the side of the car. He heard it clunk into gear and watched as the car, mere inches from his face, started to move. Just as the front tire passed him, he jumped to hide behind a large, plastic trash can. His heart pounded in his ears as he tried to calm his breathing and stay perfectly still. In a moment the door mechanism cranked again. The morning light was slowly shuttered and he was alone in silence.

Samuel stood up, his body was still shaking. With only the light that was mounted on ceiling of the garage, he looked around his surroundings. On the back wall of the garage was a tool bench with shelves above it. He walked over to the shelves, picked up a partial roll of duct tape, and worked it into his back pocket. Walking to the door that led into the house, he put a hand on the knob and, at the same time, pulled the gun out of his waistband.

Cautiously, he moved into the house. There was an eerie silence and the strong feeling that he somehow knew this house. Looking into each room to make sure no one was home, it became obvious that a family lived there. Two of the bedrooms were full of the odds and ends of adolescents. One of them displayed the clothes, teen idol posters, and pink bedspread of a girl. The other, a typical boy's room, contained the disarray of assorted sports equipment, model planes, and wallpaper with cowboys all over it. On the hallway was an array of framed photos. He started away from the pictures, then stopped. He turned his head back to the photo of a man with pleasant features. The man appeared to be in his forties. Samuel pulled the picture off the wall and looked at it closely. "Why is all this happening?" he thought, as he moved a hand over his own features. He carefully hung the photo back up, making sure that it was aligned with the others. Another photo—a pretty, smiling, middle-aged woman—caught his attention. It had to be the man's wife. A bitter sadness swept over him and tears came to his eyes. He knew her! "I'm so sorry, Karen," he said under his breath and stepped away.

At the end of the hall he entered the master bedroom. He picked up a framed family photo sitting on a nightstand. It was Timothy's family. Samuel smiled, it was the kind of family he'd wanted his whole life and just the family he would want for his own child. As quickly as it had come, the feeling of comfort was dashed away by dread. Like a dark storm cloud racing in, a black vision of hopeless horror came to his mind. Was he going to destroy yet another family? Feeling an agonizing ache in his heart, his hand shaking, he put the picture back on the nightstand and turned away. A hard determination came to his eyes—he had things to do.

At the far end of the house he found Timothy's study. There was a desk and bookshelves, all crowded with haphazardly placed books and manila folders stuffed with sheets of paper. On the desk was a small stack of paperback copies of *The Journeymen Diaries*. In the middle of the desk was a hardback copy of the book. Samuel slid the gun back into his waistband, sat down, and started quickly searching the drawers. Opening the top drawer on the right side he suddenly froze. Reaching in, he pulled out the bronze sun medallion, his hand closed on it. After a moment his eyes fell back to the open drawer.

His breath caught in his throat at the sight of a large, worn, canvas bound journal. There was no question, some part of him knew the book. He laid the medallion down on the desk and, with reverence, lifted the journal out with two hands. Opening it, his hand ran lovingly over the familiar, small, neat script. He began to turn the pages, his mind grabbing at phrases that brought everything back to him. Reading, leafing through the pages, tears rolled down his cheeks.

By the time he'd scanned over the last page, everything was clear to him. He reached into the pocket of his sweat jacket and pulled out the pen Jessup had given him at the institute. He took a sheet of blank paper from Timothy's desktop and began writing.

TIMOTHY GODWIN SAT IN A CHAIR next to Detective Rodney Jenkins' desk. His face haggard from the previous night's drinking, he sipped black coffee from a plastic cup. The detective's room was too small for all the desks crowded into it. Most of the desks sat empty. The only activity was on the other side of the room where two detectives sat talking quietly over a fast food breakfast.

"Here ya' go, Mr. Godwin," Detective Jenkins said, coming up behind him. Jenkins was stout with a strong chin, his kind, but hard eyes had the look of having seen it all. His gold badge was clipped to his belt. He set the stack of binders he was carrying on the side of the desk in front of Timothy and gave them a pat with his hand. "I need you to go through these mugshot albums, I doubt your kid's in here, but you never know." He looked at his watch. "We should have a sketch artist in here soon."

Timothy looked at the stack of albums and winced. Raising his eyebrows, he sighed in a somewhat reluctant acceptance of the task before him. He picked up the first volume.

Jenkins moved behind his desk, sat down in the chair, and leaned back. He caught Timothy's eyes with a hard, examining stare. "Are you sure you don't have any idea who this kid could be?" he asked.

Timothy looked at him blankly and shook his head. "No. I don't have a clue. Why?"

"You didn't see him hanging around at another signing? Didn't get any threatening letters or strange phone calls?"

"No. I mean . . . there's people who . . . well, you know . . . have seen me on TV . . . and, well . . . , some of them think they kind of know me, because of that. Sometimes, they can be somewhat intrusive, even a little rude," Timothy said and shook his head again. "But, no . . . nothing strange or threatening."

"He had you dead." Jenkins leaned forward and put his elbows on the desk, his brawny, cop face close to Timothy's. "There wasn't anything to stop him from shooting you except himself. He must have been pretty pissed off at you . . . to come after you with a gun. It sounds to me . . . this kid *does* know who you are." He paused, keeping the hard stare on Timothy's eyes for a long moment before he said, "Why is it that you are not using your real name? Wasn't your real name good enough for the book—Mr. Lewis?"

Timothy was surprised at the sound of his real name and the force of Jenkins stare made him blink. "Well . . . ," he said, "my father . . . , Frank Lewis. He died. After a few years, my mother remarried. Her last name is Godwin, now. I liked the sound of it and I *wanted* to use a pen name to write under . . . that's all." His eyes met the officers and his voice became stronger. "People have a right to have a private life, Detective."

Jenkins nodded, the eyes still suspicious, and patted the stack again.

Timothy picked up the first book, put it in his lap, and opened it.

SAMUEL WAS WALKING, PACING around Timothy's house. He had to think. There was too much at stake for him to make another mistake—too many lives could be put in harm's way. He was startled by the sudden rumbling of the garage door opening. Quickly, he hurried down the hallway and pressed himself against the wall in the boy's bedroom. Pulling the gun out of his waistband he waited and listened. The garage door rumbled again and, in a minute, he could hear Timothy come into the house. He listened to the footfalls coming down short hallway from the garage to the kitchen. There was silence for a few seconds, Samuel was sure he was on the carpeted floor of the living room. His straining ears were startled by a loud, jingling that sounded like bells falling onto the floor. Samuel realized before he could calm down that it was the ringtone of Timothy's cell phone.

"Hello," he heard Timothy say. "Oh, hi, Tasha, how are you?" There was a pause. "No, I'm fine . . . It shook me up a bit at the time, but I haven't seen the kid again. I'm not too worried about it. He looked just as scared as I was when he ran off." Timothy fell silent, listening. "Oh . . . ahhh, sure," he said, cheerfully. "We'll meet at seven, instead of six . . . No problem . . . great, see you then . . . at the university. Looking forward to it, I'm very curious to know what else you've translated from the manuscripts." After another pause, Timothy said, "Great, see you then, and, hey, thanks again." He hung up the phone.

Samuel inched out of the bedroom and down the hallway. For an instant, he stood still at the end of the darkened hall, peeked out, and saw Timothy put his phone down on the kitchen table. As Timothy started to unbutton his shirt, Samuel came in closer.

"You have no idea what you've done," Samuel said calmly.

Timothy literally jumped and whirled around to look squarely into the barrel of the pistol pointed at his head. "You!" he said, his face white in shock.

Samuel felt a pang of sympathy, he didn't want to scare Timothy, but he couldn't leave any room for him to think he wasn't deadly serious. He motioned with the pistol for him to move. "Your study," he said, "let's go."

Instinctively holding his hands up, Timothy started walking toward the hallway that led to the other end of the house. "Wha . . . what . . . do you want?" he stammered, "I don't even know you."

Entering the study Samuel tossed the duct tape at Timothy. "Get in the chair," he said, motioning with the gun. In obvious fear, Timothy sat down. "Tape your ankles together and one wrist to the arm of the chair. Run the tape around several times. Don't try to fool me with a half-assed job."

When Timothy was finished, Samuel grabbed the duct tape from him and laid the pistol down on a bookshelf. "Don't try and move from the chair or do anything stupid."

Timothy blinked and nodded his head several times.

"Just do what I say. You don't have to get hurt in this," Samuel said. He grabbed Timothy's free wrist and taped it down to the other arm of the chair.

"Why are you doing this?" Timothy asked.

"You can relax, Tim. I'm not the one you need to be afraid of."

Timothy raised his eyebrows. "So, *who* is it that I should be afraid of?" he asked, his voice, high pitched now, running on in fear. "You're the one that's held a gun to my head *twice* and, now, broken into my house. I haven't done anything to you, I—"

"You need to understand what you've done, Tim."

"What I've done? I did something to you?" Timothy's eyes searched Samuel's face wildly.

"Calm down and listen," Samuel said. "You have published my memoirs and altered an accurate account of two incarnates that have fought against one another for centuries."

"Your memoirs?" Timothy said incredulously.

"Yes, my memories," Samuel said nodding. He walked around and sat on a corner of the desk. "Incarnates have no memory of their previous lives, at least not until something reminds them of the past or who they've been. After I read your book, I began to remember all the things I had forgotten. It was confusing at first because of all the changes you made to my notes." He paused and gave Timothy an amused smile. "Then everything kind of settled in and became clear."

Timothy shook his head. "No," he said, "it's just a story."

Samuel's eyes narrowed. "A story! I didn't kill myself at Fort Saint Mark, next to Loxton," he said, his voice, for the first time, edged with anger. The memory was there, flashing crystal clear pictures in Samuels's mind. He took a deep breath and exhaled, calming himself. "Maybe you'll understand if I tell you what really happened, Tim. Tell you what I know that you've changed . . . and that you have put yourself and your family in the middle of real danger."

CHAPTER SIXTEEN

SEBASTIAN LOXTON, HIS HORSE AT A GALLUP, pulled up as he rode into the woodland clearing. His lip curled in distaste at the sight before him, dead men scattered about the clearing and into the edges of the woods—dead men in the scarlet uniform of the British army. His eyes then turned to the few bodies of colonists that were scattered amongst the dead. Staying mounted, his horse snorting and breathing heavily, he moved through the carnage, examining each corpse. The anger etched in his face grew sharper as he searched. Finally, he raised his head and looked into the tangled wall of forest that surrounded him. "Go! Go on, Victor," he yelled. "You will find the blood of your family still warm!" He pulled on the reins leading the horse around and galloped away, eastward on the path that led back towards the settlement of Saint Augustine and the sea.

Nearing the fortress, Sebastian was riding hard around a bend when his eyes widened in surprise. A figure, a man, was standing in the path with a sword in hand. Sebastian pulled his sword, spurred his horse and raced forward. Closer, a snarl of pleasure came to his face. It was Victor, sword at the ready, his feet apart and crouching slightly, he was ready to fight. Nearing him, Sebastian raised his sword high above his head.

Scowling in defiance, Victor stood his ground. Waiting until the last instant, his free hand shot out from behind his back, holding a pistol. He aimed carefully, fired, and made a diving roll for the side of the road.

The bullet struck Sebastian's shoulder. Recoiling from the sharp pain, he dropped his sword and pulled in tightly on the horse's reins. The stallion lost its footing, whinnied, and fell instantly, collapsing to the ground.

Victor, scrambling to his feet, watched as the animal fell into a rolling flip, throwing Sebastian forward high into the air and onto the path. The entire weight of the horse came smashing down on its rider before rolling on another twenty feet. Whinnying in distress, the animal scrambled to his feet and galloped away.

Sword in hand, Victor raced to stand over his foe. Sebastian's crushed and mangled body laid motionless, arms and legs bent and broken, blood pouring from his nose and mouth. The only sign of life was his pain stricken eyes staring up at the open sky. Slowly, the eyes moved to Victor's face.

"Finish it," Loxton demanded, straining to get the words out.

Victor looked down at him with raw hatred. "No," he said. "No, I want to watch you suffer." He reached down under the collar of Sebastian's shirt, his fingers found the chain of a necklace. Breaking the chain, he ripped it free. It was the bronze sun medallion.

"Just something to remember you by," Victor scorned. He watched as Sebastian, his body shaking in uncontrollable spasms, struggled to breathe. In less than a minute, the blood gushing into the mouth was too much. Sebastian gagged and coughed, spewing sprays of red into the air. Gasping, drowning in his own blood, he died.

A satisfaction came to Victor's face. He stood, backed away, and watched as a shimmering vapor seeped from Sebastian's corpse. It gathered, swirling over the body, pushing and moving within itself, forming into a ghostly apparition. Fierce, glowing eyes appeared, burning out from above, the mouth set in the evil, grin of death.

Facing the entity, Victor swore, "I *will* find you again."

Almost as soon as Sebastian's demonic soul fully formed, it screeched loudly and instantly evaporated, exploding outward in all directions.

Turning his back, Victor walked away.

Later, at twilight, the waning light filtered in through the open door of the mausoleum. Victor opened the old, ironwood chest and placed the sun medallion inside, on top of a collection of ancient parchments and scrolls. Stepping out of the mausoleum, he pulled the door closed and locked it with the spool-key.

Walking into the night, guided by a full moon, he made his way back to his cabin. He immediately started digging. By first light he'd finished burying his wife and children. In the small, open work shed he fashioned three oaken crosses. With the end of a shovel he hammered one into each of the freshly filled graves. Breathing hard from his labors, he stood for several minutes in crushing agony. He fell to his knees, head down, and clasped his hands in prayer. Finishing his silent grieving, he looked up at the sky. His eyes turned to the sword that lay in the dirt beside him. He picked it up, holding the hilt above his head, and placing the tip against his abdomen. Stilling his labored breathing, he closed his eyes, and without hesitation thrust the sword through his body. Quivering in pain, he jerked the hilt along his waist, quickening his death.

AS SAMUEL FINISHED TELLING TIMOTHY GODWIN what had actually happened to Victor—what was really written in the journal—he could still read the disbelief in his mind.

"*You're* Victor?" Timothy scoffed. "I don't how long you've been here, but apparently long enough to go through my stuff!"

Samuel stood, turned the chair to face him, and leaned into Timothy's face, his hands on his captive's bound wrists. "Hear me out, Tim," he said. "Because of what you've published, Loxton is going to come looking for you, just as I have. He'll want to know why you know so much and you won't be able to hide anything from him. Once an incarnate begins to awaken, they're able to look into someone's eyes and see them for who they really are." Samuel leaned in even closer and drew out his words for emphasis. "He'll read you like a book." He stood up. "I'm sorry I left that journal, Tim. I had no intention of you ever finding it . . . or anything else."

Samuel saw the confusion, the questions in Timothy's mind. "I wrote that journal to keep a record of my dreams—nightmares—not knowing they were memories." He looked into Timothy's eyes. "I was murdered eighteen years ago after I found the memoirs I had written, and hidden, during previous lives, to help me remember who I had been. They are my history, a history that has been recorded over thousands of years." He fell silent and waited, watching Timothy's eyes. Seeing into his mind he saw him struggle with believing, trying to make some sense of it all. "Before I died, I remember putting them, along with a bronze sun medallion, into a leather bag. The bag had a Coptic cross engraved on it."

"You're telling me, *you* wrote those?"

Samuel nodded. "Yes."

Timothy shook his head. "No, that can't be right. How could you know . . . ?"

Samuel spoke calmly, "I told you, I was murdered. I was born into this body the day I died, August, tenth, nineteen ninety-two. My name was Frank Lewis." He watched the light come on in Timothy's eyes.

"Frank Lewis! No," Timothy said, his voice quavering. "You're telling me that you are my father?"

Samuel smiled at him. He watched Timothy's mind begin to go through rapid cycles of confusion—fighting the possibility it could be true.

Timothy's eyes moistened and there was a flash of anger. "If you're my father why have you tied me to this chair?"

"I'm trying to save your life, Tim."

"And leaving me taped to this chair is going to do that?"

"Perhaps. I heard you on the phone, talking to Tasha," Samuel said and gave Timothy a narrowed, sidelong gaze. "I doubt anyone other than Loxton could have translated my work. Just exactly where would I find her?"

Timothy gave him a dismissive grunt of a laugh before, suddenly, his eyes widened. "Wait, wait, you think that Tasha is Loxton? That's ridiculous!"

"Ridiculous?" Samuel asked. "Would any of this I've told you make any sense in most people's frame of reference? I won't know for sure until I see her. But, if she is . . . I'll kill her." He watched the color drain from Timothy's face. "I can't have you standing in the way, or be a part of this, any more than you already are." Samuel stood up and started for the door, then came back and put his face close to Timothy's again. "I know you're having trouble believing any of this . . . and I don't know if I'll see you again in this life, Tim, but . . . I . . . hope things go well for you and your family. I'm sorry for all I've put you through and . . . your mother too. I didn't know who I was at the time." He turned quickly and walked out of the room.

"Hey!" Timothy called, "wait . . . you can't leave me tied up!" With the sound of the front door opening he yelled, "For God's sake you can't just kill an innocent woman!"

TASHA SAT BEHIND THE DESK in her university office translating Timothy's documents. She was spending more and more of her time working on them. Going over a passage, she read aloud to herself, "They are watched and heard from above and below, for should they forget whom they serve, judgment shall come swiftly."

In the hallway, approaching the open door to her office, Samuel paused. A nagging uncertainty for the woman's life—and, his own responsibility—had been eating at him. Still, he steeled himself with the overwhelming, compulsive certainty of who he was about to face and what he would have to do. "No matter the earthly form, it doesn't change anything," he said to himself. Gritting his teeth, he stepped into the open doorway.

Tasha, her gloved finger moving along the lines of script, didn't look up. Samuel eyes focused on her with a sharp stare. He froze in disbelief and quickly backed himself into the hallway, moving against the wall, and out of sight. He was wrong. She wasn't the one. He had been wrong twice now, putting innocent people's lives in danger. Exhaling, he stepped quietly back into the room.

Continuing to read aloud, Tasha read, "They wander through each life in darkness until a sign sheds light. Should their paths cross in any life . . ."

"The past will be revealed," Samuel said aloud, finishing her sentence.

Tasha looked up in surprise. Samuel was standing in front of her, staring into her eyes. She swallowed hard and her face contorted in concern, shaken at the animal-like intensity of his stare. No words came to her.

"I'm sorry that I startled you," Samuel said. "My name is Samuel. I'm here for the manuscripts."

"How did you get in here?" she asked, her voice was unable to hide her fear. "You can't just . . ."

Samuel held up a hand, signaling her to stop.

Tasha could only look at him blankly, her eyes continually darting toward the door as though looking or hoping for someone to intervene.

"Shall I tell you what you *really* want to know?" Samuel asked.

Her mouth fell open as she tried to say something, but couldn't.

"Keep in mind, Tasha," Samuel continued, "that the more you know, the more you place yourself at risk. Is knowledge that valuable to you?" He could see her still frightened eyes trying to think, weighing what he was saying.

Tasha cleared her throat. "Only if it's the truth," she managed.

"Very well. I know the text in that script because I wrote it two-thousand years ago."

It took Tasha a moment to digest what he'd said. Finally, she challenged him. "If you wrote this, then who are the two that it's written about?" she asked, her hands indicating the documents that covered her desktop.

"One is the man that committed the first evil," Samuel answered, looking her straight in the eyes. Reading her, he could see that she was missing the mark. "Don't confuse it with the first sin, Tasha."

"So, then. Wha . . . what would this first evil have been?" she asked.

He could see that she believed that he was the one who'd threatened Timothy at the bookstore and that she was very frightened. "Murder," Samuel said, letting the weight of the word fall in the silence of the room.

"And the other?" Tasha asked.

Samuel opened his hands in front of her. "Stands before you," he said. "I was the victim."

CHAPTER SEVENTEEN

ABLE, A GOAT-SKIN LOINCLOTH COVERING HIM, knelt in reverence, his forehead on the ground before the crude, hilltop stone altar. He raised his head enough to look up in reverent petition at the white smoke rising into the air from the smoldering carcass of a lamb. Bowing his head, he prayed. "Lord, God, accept my offering that I may be blessed to receive a bounty from the coming season." Impatiently he again peeked up at the altar and added, "If it should please you to do so, Lord." He softly mumbled a repetitive chant for several minutes, before he rose to his feet, bowed his head, turned, and started away. Coming down the path he met his older brother, Cain. The two nodded at one another and passed without words.

Cain, carrying a basket brimming with fruit and vegetables, stopped and looked back to watch his brother descend toward his flock in the field below. The muscles of Cain's jaw twitched at the sight of the healthy sheep moving across the bright, green grass. He sighed, lowered his head and continued on to a second, stone altar that was set only a few yards from his brother's. Lifting the basket, his heart sank. Was it worthy of a righteous god, of whom he asked so much? "It is all I have, Lord," he said. With a guilty look, he placed the basket on the altar. The instant he set it down, there was a bright, blinding flash. The force of it was so great that it knocked Cain to the ground. Lying on the grass, he cowered in fear. His offering had burst into a hot, white flame, sending black bellows of smoke straight up into the air. He crawled away for a distance then slowly brought himself to his feet. The offering had disappeared; in its place was only smoldering, black ash. Shaken, he backed away.

Able came running up the hill and grabbed his brother's shoulders. He shook him, and demanded, "What have you done?"

Cain's eyes filled with hate. He knocked Able's hands away and stormed off down the hill.

Hurt and confusion knotted Cain's face as he chopped weeds around the seedlings in his garden. He had worked for hours, nonstop. Every so often the pain in his heart would be so great that he would stop, look up at the sky, and ask, "Why, Lord?" Exhausted, the sun mercilessly beating down on him, he looked down at his blistered and calloused hands. They were so stiff that when he tried to open them they cracked and bled. Feeling defeated, he looked off into the distance, where he saw Able standing at ease, leaning on his staff, while tending his flock. At the sight, a great, uncontrollable anger came over him and he began walking toward his brother.

As Cain approached his brother, resentment and hate swelled inside of him to where it became unbearable. Able, lost in caring for his flock, had no awareness of his brother's approach. Stepping up behind him, Cain raised his hoe and swung it with all his strength into the back of his brother's head. Able fell like a stone. His brother stood watching the blood pour from the lifeless body into the earth. Realizing what he'd done he grew frightened, turned, and ran.

For the rest of the morning and into the afternoon, Cain worked his field, hoeing with the same tool that he'd used to slay his brother. But he felt something. Something was different, as though there was a change in the light of day or the smell of the air. He fidgeted, looking about nervously. At times, he would suddenly whirl around in panic, thinking someone was coming up behind him. Trying to ignore the feelings, he put his fear into his hoe, sweating and breathing hard, until finally he'd had too much. Someone, he was sure, was watching him. He looked, turning full around and saw no one. He raised a fearful eye to the sky.

"Am I to watch over my brother," he cried aloud.

A sudden, angry, cutting wind came down from the north, ripping across the grass, bringing forth scattered debris and dust. Cain, shielding his fear widened eyes, dropped his hoe to the ground. He watched as the clouds turned dark and the sun blackened. He covered his head with his hands and lowered his eyes.

At Cain's feet, droplets of red blood began seeping up, out of the ground. In seconds it was coming faster, bubbling from the soil. It came faster still, rising to where it washed over his sandals and between his toes. He shivered with terror at the blood and started backing slowly away. Losing his footing, he tripped, falling to the ground into the hot, sticky blood. He scrambled to his feet and frantically tried to wipe the blood from his body. To his horror he saw that it would not come off. It bled into his own skin, coursing through his veins and stained his body from the inside. He stilled himself and looked up to the sky, his teeth bared in fierce anger. "No!!!!" he screamed into the heavens. As quickly as the word left his mouth a lightning bolt exploded from the sky, striking into his face, knocking him to the ground. He floundered violently.

As swiftly as the storm had come—it was gone. Dazed, Cain slowly revived. He looked around in fearful suspicion before he leapt to his feet and ran to his small, stone house. Taking only his walking staff and a few crusts of bread, he left his land forever.

For many years, he wandered in the wilderness. His face was scarred from the lightning and his body permanently stained with the blood of his brother. He became an old man, wrinkled and ravaged by time and rigors of his travels. Unkempt gray hair from his head and beard had grown to his waist.

There came a day when, parched and starving to near death, Cain found himself struggling through endless, barren, sand dunes. Finally at the top of a dune, in the near distance, he saw green— trees and grass lined the bank of a river. With all of his remaining energy he rushed to the river and waded in until his body was submerged in the cool, clear water.

Rising from the water, refreshed, he saw that a group of villagers had gathered on the far bank. Their eyes stared warily at the strange old man, bearing a burn mark on his face and blood stained skin. Fearful, the men of the tribe bent and armed themselves with large stones and, with their arms drawn back to throw, waded into the river, coming slowly toward him.

Waist deep in the water, Cain stood to his full height and, holding his wooden staff, raised his arms straight up above his head. "Know who I am!" he commanded. "Any man that slay me shall suffer sevenfold!"

The men stopped for a moment, looked at each other uncertainly, and then came forward again.

In a loud, deep, tone of authority, Cain said, "I am Cain!"

The men stopped in their tracks. The stones falling from their hands, they backed away. Cain let out a roaring laugh that sent them scattering like frightened children.

Cain settled in the village, becoming a feared and prosperous man who took whatever he wanted from his neighbors. He lived for many more years. In great age he went to his death bed and waited. During the night, he awakened from a restless sleep. His eyes, bleary with age and his oncoming death, made out a shadowy figure standing at the foot of his bed. The visage was long and slender, and did not appear to be clothed. The creature stepped closer, moving slowly with a sensuous and, somehow, alluringly evil grace. Cain could not help but feel a physical attraction to the subtle curves of the creature's body even though he could not tell if it was a man or a woman.

"Who are you?" he demanded, trying to blink the vision from his eyes. "What are you . . . and why are you here?

The creature spoke in a voice that was low, drawn out, and seductive. It seemed to come from a great depth and echoed with the sound of many voices at once. "I am neither man, woman, nor beast. I am what I choose to be. And, I have come here for you. You've done well for yourself, Cain. You have brought forth civilization. I," it said, edging on an evil laughter, "find this very pleasing . . . bringing earthly desires to man, adding to his own, natural desires of the flesh." The creature gave out a low hiss and, suddenly, leapt into the air like a great, vile insect. It landed on the edge of the bed, and moving with slithering seduction, made its way up against Cain's body.

Cain looked into creature's alluring, mesmerizing eyes and found himself powerless. "What do you want of me?" he demanded.

There was a deep, gurgle of a chuckle from the creature. "What do I want from you?" it said. In the flash of an instant, it was suddenly on its haunches, straddling Cain's hips. Swaying its body seductively, it lowered itself down to lay against the dying man's chest. Raising its head, red eyes fierce and glowing, its breath the unmistakable stench of death, it spoke again. "You committed murder, Cain. Your soul belongs to me and tonight you'll die and find yourself in Hell."

Cain's eyes widened; such a creature could only be the Devil. He stared into the fiercely evil eyes in disbelief as the creature undulated against him. To his great horror he found the seduction irresistible. Unable to speak, he said nothing.

Suddenly, the Devil stilled and bent his face almost touching Cain's. "I can," it said, "give you one more chance to live among the flesh, but . . . you will do my bidding."

The words came to Cain like a snake crawling over his heart. "What?" he gasped. "What do you want of me?"

With its eyes burning into Cain's, the Devil's voice hissed. "To fill Hell with every living soul on Earth. My bidding is that you lure man away from the Divine and from his own spirit. Make him suffer if he doesn't do your will. In return, you'll be given life, to pursue and fulfill all your worldly desires . . . for many lives to come. I will lead you unto your enemies, that you may defeat them. Defy me and you will suffer far more than any that fall before you." With that the Devil smiled. Lowering its head, it opened its mouth and placed it hard over Cain's lips. Inhaling a long, powerful breath, it filled its lungs with Cain's soul. Sitting up on Cain's now lifeless body, the Devil arched its back. Looking straight up, the unholy creature heaved with a long, shattering growl, and, in a stream of white, ghostly mist, spat Cain's soul out into the air. The Devil licked its lips with a long, red tongue as it watched the mist gather above. The shapeless soul lingered for only an instant, before it dissipated into nothing. The Devil let out a blood-stilling cackle, knowing a child had drawn its first breath and Cain was again born into the world.

BOUND TO THE CHAIR, TIMOTHY GODWIN was startled by the melodic chime of his front door bell. After a brief wave of apprehension, his face brightened in realization. If his captor came back he wouldn't be ringing the door bell.

"Help!" Timothy cried, "help me!" There was the pounding of footsteps coming down the hallway.

Nathan Kibbling burst into the room. "What the . . ." He reached down, his hands worked to find the ends of the duct tape.

"Scissors. In the top drawer," Timothy said.

Nathan went to the drawer and pulled out the scissors. "The kid, right?" he asked. "What did he do? I knew you should have stayed with me. Are you okay?" He carefully started to work the scissors under the duct tape. "My God, he could have killed you!"

"Yeah, yeah, I'm fine. Thank God you showed up!"

"Are you injured?"

In his excitement, Timothy's words came out in a rush. "No. He didn't do anything to hurt me. He just told me things."

"What sort of things?" Nathan stopped working the scissors and looked at him.

"He said he was Frank."

"What?"

"I know it sounds crazy, but the kid . . . said he was Frank . . . , my father."

"Are you sure? That doesn't make sense."

"Nathan, he believes he's an incarnate."

"What? You mean like in your book?"

"For God's sake, Nathan, cut the damn tape will you?"

"Yes, I am. You don't want your arm cut off, do you?"

"Please, just hurry," Timothy said. "The kid said the manuscripts aren't just stories—they're archives about two real incarnates. He thinks he's one of them and now he's gone after Tasha . . . thinking that she's the other."

Nathan stopped working the scissors. An amused look came to his face. "Tasha?" he said. "Then he'll be coming back for you." Nathan stood up and tossed the scissors on a shelf of the bookcase behind him.

Timothy looked at him in confusion then looked down at his bound arms. "What are you doing? Cut the damn tape, will you?"

Nathan only looked at him with cold contempt. "I knew it," he said. "I knew your book would awaken him and lure him out."

"Wha . . . no," Timothy said. "Surely, you don't . . ." Timothy stared up at him, in apprehension and fear. "You were using me . . . to lure him? This is insane—you can't be telling me *you're* Loxton?

Distracted, lost in his own thoughts, Nathan shrugged. "So many names. So many lives. He looked toward the sunlight poking out of the edges of the closed window blinds, his eyes glazed over as though he were peering into another place and another time.

CHAPTER EIGHTTEEN

NATHAN KIBBLING DROVE THROUGH THE DARKNESS, compelled by instinct. The very same instinct that had lead him since his birth had him out, urging him to drive halfway across the state in the middle of the night. The very purpose of his existence beckoned him toward what he had to do on this night. Staring at the two-lane road that led to the coast and Saint Augustine, something ahead caught his eye.

Off on the on the shoulder of the road, were a pair of yellow blinking lights. There were two cars, one parked behind the other, with a man leaning over, loading a tire into an open trunk. Nathan's dark eyes fell on a faint, but obvious glowing blue aura that emanated from the man. Closer still, the man closed the trunk and glanced, squinting into the oncoming headlights of Nathan's car. A burning, white glow came from the man's eyes. The glow cut into Nathan's soul like a red hot blade. A cold, black hatred washed over him as he sped by. The hatred grew to a terrible, consuming, cold rage that was beyond thought and reason. There was no thought, conclusion or plan—he didn't need any—it was as it had been since the beginning.

A few hundred yards down the road Nathan's headlights picked up a farm road off to the left. He braked, nosed into it, and backed out, turning the car around. Ahead, the man walked up to the driver's side window and leaned in to talk to the woman sitting behind the wheel. Nathan eased the car forward, slowly gaining speed. Closing on the man, he suddenly stomped on the gas pedal. The engine roared and the tires screeched. Nathan's eyes were fixed in a chilling, demonic stare, emanating a sense of fulfillment.

The man on the side of the road looked up at the sound of the racing engine. The pleasant smile on his face fell to a look of concern as he tried to shade the glare of the oncoming headlights with a hand. He straightened as though readying himself to move, but it was too late.

At the last instant, Nathan yanked the steering wheel toward the man. The car slammed into the woman's car with a loud, scraping rasp. The body of the man was caught between the cars, crushed from the impact, and sent flying into the air. It landed lifeless on the asphalt. A rapidly spreading pool of blood began to form around his head.

Nathan, driving away, looking in the rearview mirror, felt a sense of pleasure at the sight of the crumpled body of the man he'd just murdered. He adjusted the mirror to look at himself, smiling demonically. "He must have stopped to help the woman," he said aloud, and laughed. That made it all especially sweet. "In the words of Clare Booth Luce . . . 'No good deed goes unpunished.'"

STANDING IN TIMOTHY'S STUDY, Nathan remained transfixed, staring at the light seeping by the edge of the blind.

Timothy was still looking at him with apprehension and fear. "I want nothing more to do with this," he said, his voice taking on a pleading tone. "Please, let me go . . . I won't call the police . . . or tell anyone."

"Let you go," Nathan said, casting him with a dark, hideous glare. "I'm not even close to being through with you yet. I murdered your father and, now, I'm going to murder him again. Thanks to you he has made his way back to where I've wanted him all along." He turned as though he was going to leave, then whirled around, and exploded a hard right-hand to Timothy's jaw. Timothy's head snapped back from the force of the blow and he sagged forward into unconsciousness.

SAMUEL COULD READ IT CLEARLY in Tasha's eyes. While she was intrigued by his recount of Cain and Able, she couldn't bring herself to believe what he was saying. She was still very afraid of him. "You don't believe me," he said.

Looking at him, she hesitated. "I didn't say that."

"You didn't have to." He stepped closer, right up to her desk and held out his hand. "May I have the Sumerian text please?"

"Look these are valuable antiquities," she said. "They can't be subjected to someone just wandering in off the street and rifling through them."

Samuel smiled reassuringly. "I'll be very careful with them," he promised. Reaching down, he gently picked up the Sumerian documents from the stack. His eyes scanned as he turned the pages. "In your opinion, Dr. Eldridge, how many eighteen-year-olds can translate Sumerian?" He looked at her and smiled. "That is, eighteen-year-olds that wander in off the street just to rifle through them." He pointed to a word in the text. "Translate from here, please."

Taking a deep long breath and letting it out slowly, Tasha read aloud, "First born."

"Yes . . . , continue," he requested.

"Slain," she said.

"And here," said Samuel, pointing to another part of the page.

"Herdsmen," she answered.

"No, 'Shepherd,'" he corrected. "A significant difference from 'herdsman.' One of considerable importance at the time it was written."

Tasha looked up at him. "Yes . . . , of course," she said, "you're right, actually," she said, a puzzled look on her face. She shook her head from side to side as though shaking away any possibility that what he was saying was true. "Look, just because you know this text, doesn't mean that you were Able, or that these documents relate true facts. I don't believe . . ."

"Belief is not knowing, Tasha," he said. "One thing I've learned over the centuries is that people are going to believe what they are taught to believe, what they want to believe, and what they are willing to believe. I have no time to try and convince you of who I am." He paused and looked into her eyes. "You're thinking that I'm suffering from a severe psychosis." He smiled. "I assure you, that I've had enough psychological evaluations to last me through another century."

Tasha's eyes widened in embarrassment. "I . . . I didn't say that," she snapped.

Samuel laid the document back down and leaned toward her with his hands on her desk. "Look doctor, what's important right now is that Cain is out there somewhere. He *is* an incarnate of evil and has been responsible for the deaths of millions. He has tortured and murdered innocent men, women, and children, without any remorse since the beginning of mankind. You have *no* idea of what he is capable of. I've seen his wrath and when he finds out . . ." Samuel stopped himself. It had suddenly come to him. In realization, he began to think out loud. "He knows about the book. That's why the anhangers were in Saint Augustine.

Waiting. He sent them. There's no other way they could have known."

"What?" Tasha asked.

"I'm running out of time," Samuel said. "He knows about Timothy's book. He'll track him down just like I did, wanting to know why he knows so much. And when he finds him . . ." He gave Tasha a sobering look, "he'll kill him."

"Why would he kill Timothy Godwin?"

"Because, Timothy is my son," Samuel answered, "that's why." For the first time, Samuel could see Tasha's mind open to allow herself to believe that he might be telling the truth. He watched in silence as, for the first time, the fear in her eyes subsided.

AS TASHA DROVE, SAMUEL STARED OUT the front passenger side window of her car. His mind took no notice of the sparse, evening traffic. He was lost in thought desperately trying to figure out what he should do next.

Tasha broke the silence. "You went after Timothy, thinking he was Cain. And then you came after me . . . thinking the same thing." She gave Samuel a quick, nervous glance. "You don't know where to go from here . . . do you?"

At the sound of her voice, Samuel turned and looked at her, he wasn't sure he wanted her to know more than she already did. He hesitated a second before he took a deep breath and exhaled. "No," he said, "I don't. But Cain's no fool. He will find Timothy and then he'll find you too, just like I did."

"How is it that you found me?"

"It's only a matter of asking the right question. I'm able to preserve whatever comes to someone's mind, when looking into their eyes. Timothy wasn't able to hide you from me. The two of you will have to go into hiding until this is over."

"Hiding! Until this is over? What is that supposed to mean?"

Samuel wasn't sure what to say. He tried to find something that would ease her fears, make all of this seem more bearable—less life threatening. But he was not able to find anything that wouldn't be an outright lie and make it even more dangerous for her.

"Samuel," Tasha said, her voice was calm and soft, like she was trying to soothe him, "please help me to understand something. Maybe I can help you. One of the Greek texts said that . . . , 'they will know one another by the eyes of fire, the burning beyond the skin; the end is near, a time for a new beginning.' What does all that mean?"

"Auras," answered Samuel.

"You can see people's auras?"

"No, just his . . . a fiery red glow and bright, burning white eyes. He could be standing among a thousand people, and I'd be able to spot him at a glance. We've found each other that way before."

"So, what happens then?"

"Just as it's always been. A fight to the death . . . and then on to another beginning."

"Is it like the book says . . . that you're born into the next child that draws its first breath . . . never knowing where you will be born?"

Staring intently at the approaching headlights, Samuel nodded his head slowly. "It's known to us as 'the passing' and has always been that way. But . . . I'm thinking . . . Cain may have found a way around it."

Tasha looked at him blankly. "What do you mean? He can choose who he's born into?"

Samuel turned and looked at her. "In 1945—I was in Germany, during the war—I found a woman that was dead after a cesarean had been performed on her. Her baby was the reincarnate of Cain and there were people protecting him—they knew. They knew who that baby was."

"Oh, my God," Tasha said softly, as though to herself. She shot a quick glance at Samuel. "No, not Rebecca!" She suddenly turned the steering wheel hard to the left and skidded across two lanes of traffic, making a u-turn in the middle of the street. Samuel's body was thrown against the passenger door.

"What are you doing?" he shouted. He tried to find her eyes, to read her, but she was looking straight ahead as she accelerated.

"Look, Samuel, you've got to trust me. Rebecca—she's pregnant and has refused to tell me who the father is or anything else about the baby."

"Wait . . . ," Samuel started.

"I'm sorry Samuel, but I have to know!" Tasha screamed at him, "I just hope I'm wrong!"

Tasha's car jerked to a hard stop in the driveway of her home. Racing to the front door with Samuel right behind her, she cursed while searching her purse for her keys. Finding them, she unlocked the door and the two of them ran inside.

"Rebecca!" Tasha shouted, looking around the living room. "Rebecca? I'd be surprised if she went anywhere." She started for the kitchen when Rebecca stepped quietly out from the dark hallway.

"What?" Rebecca asked. "What's wrong?" Her eyes darted fearfully towards Samuel.

"Thank God," Tasha said, throwing her arms around the girl and hugging her. She held her for a moment then stepped back with her hands on Rebecca's shoulders. "Rebecca, who is the father of your baby?"

Samuel could see the girl's face freeze in sudden panic.

Tasha gently shook her shoulders. "Rebecca, we need to know what is really going on."

The girl turned in terror and confusion, and looked at Samuel. He stared deeply into her large blue eyes and felt her fear. It was as though he was falling into her mind and could see clearly every nuance of her thoughts. He saw a memory surface in her mind: dressed in a nightshirt, Rebecca was being escorted by her mother to a doorway.

"Do this," her mother said soothingly, "and your son shall be revered by all that know him." The mother pushed open the door to the bedroom. In the dim light the figure of a man was standing next to the bed, his back to the door. Slowly, the man turned his head and looked back over his shoulder. Samuel could feel the young girls heart stop, she knows the man—it is Nathan.

With a flash of anger, Samuel looked away from Rebecca's eyes, his jaw muscles clamped tightly. Looking back, he saw something else in her eyes that she didn't want to reveal. "We need to leave right now," he said.

As they drove, Rebecca leaned forward from the back seat. "Where are we going?" she asked meekly, moving her head to try and see the eyes of Tasha, then Samuel.

Turning back to look at her, Samuel spoke gently. "To get as far away from your stepfather as possible."

"Stepfather?" Tasha said. "Nathan's not your father?"

"You have no idea what he is," Rebecca said. "He's . . ." The intensity of Samuel's stare stopped her in mid sentence.

"You not giving him a son," Samuel said, "is the least of your worries. And you know that."

"Oh, my god," Tasha said, her words dripping with disgust and anger. "I can't believe he . . . ." She stopped talking and shook her head. Looking in the mirror she saw Rebecca fall back against the seatback and cross her arms over her chest, tears rolled down the girl's cheeks.

"How could you know that?" Rebecca asked Samuel. "Who are you?"

"That's a very long story, Rebecca. But for right now, I need to know how your stepfather planned on becoming reborn into your child," Samuel said.

Rebecca stared into his eyes as though she was recognizing something. "He looks at me like that. You're like him. Aren't you? You can read people's souls."

"If you want to call it that," he said.

There was a questioning doubt on Rebecca's face. "He said he was the only one . . . do you come back from the dead too?"

He nodded.

"Honey," Tasha said, "Nathan's not the man he's led you to believe he is."

Samuel was staring at the girl again. "Deep down you already know that." He watched Rebecca's childlike eyes well with tears.

The girl looked down, then, looked up again, wiping at her eyes with her hands. "He calls it 'the passing,'" she said. "We were to be . . . sealed inside a chamber."

The words jolted Samuel's memory as vision struck him of the Fleischgeworden in a black cloak and a skeletal mask, lying in an iron vault.

"When it came time for the baby to be born . . . ," she said with a sob, "before it drew its first breath."

Samuel replayed the ancestral memory that had become as sharp as his own: the cloaked figure in the vault pulling an ornate dagger, the sun medallion on the hilt. With both hands he placed the point of the knife against his chest and forced it violently into his own heart. Samuel blinked, his eyes cleared and he could hear Rebecca talking again.

"He was to take his own life . . . freeing his soul to become the baby's first breath."

"What sort of chamber, Rebecca?" Tasha asked.

"It's like an iron chamber in the floor that you can step down into. It creeps me out, just looking down into it," Rebecca said.

"Oh, boy," Tasha said, taking a deep breath and, puffing her cheeks, she let it out slowly.

"What is it?" Samuel asked.

"The Sumerian text, on one of the oldest documents in the collection. 'For those whom death never falls, that are not unlike the devil . . .'"

". . . shall be bound by chains and shackles of iron, to be free no more," Samuel said, completing the passage.

"His soul," Tasha said, "it can't pass through iron. He's using it to his advantage." She gave him a hopeful look. "But, that also means . . . he can be trapped. Right?"

"Yes," Samuel answered. He paused and turned to look out into the dark, focusing as though he were trying to see a great distance. "But . . . so can I."

"No, Samuel. I don't think so. It said,' not unlike the devil.' That is to be evil. You've fought against evil for eons."

Samuel looked away. "I've lived many lives, Tasha," he said, "I assure you, I'm no saint."

SAMUEL, TASHA, AND REBECCA ran down the hallway of Timothy's home and into his study. Immediately, Samuel knew that something was very wrong. The man duct taped to the chair had a black hood over his head and slumped forward against his restraints as though unconscious. It obviously wasn't Timothy Godwin.

"How could you do this?" Tasha said to Samuel. She put a protective arm around Rebecca and they took a step back toward the hallway.

"I didn't," Samuel said. "Someone else was here."

Just as he started to reach out to remove the head covering, the figure moved and a frightened, muffled voice came from beneath the hood. "Who's there?"

Samuel put a hand on the hood. At his touch, the man jerked his head away and thrashed about as violently as the bounds would allow. "No!" he screamed in terror. "Nooooo!!!!"

"It's okay," Samuel said, loudly. He put his hands on the captive's shoulders. "I'm not going to hurt you."

Suddenly, the figure went still and turned his hooded head upward. "Sam!" he asked, desperate hope sounded in his voice.

It was Calvin. Samuel began untying the hood.

"S-S-am," Calvin stuttered, "is th-that you?"

"Yeah, it's me," Samuel said, "it's okay, you're safe." He gently pulled off the hood. Calvin's face was covered with bruises and cuts, his eyes were swollen almost completely shut. He was almost unrecognizable. Samuel knelt and started tearing at the duct tape. Tasha rushed over to help.

"I'm so sorry, Cal, I thought you'd be safe." Samuel said. A sickening, sorrow welled up in his stomach and caught in his throat.

"Well, Sam, you were right about one thing," Calvin said, his swollen and bloody lips gave the hint of a smile then winced in pain.

"What's that, Cal?"

"I'm not getting to see you again, in this life." Calvin managed a weak, barely audible chuckle. "I can't see a damn thing."

Samuel smiled and put a hand on Calvin's shoulder. "We're gonna get you out of here, man. You're gonna be okay."

"Sam?" Calvin said.

"Yeah?"

"I was left here to give you a message." Calvin paused, trying to maintain his composure. Tears rolled down his face from the swollen slits that were his eyes and his lips trembled.

Samuel patted his shoulder. "It's okay, go ahead."

"I-I've got to get this right. You are to be at the Thomas Center, Spanish Court . . . ten o'clock." Calvin paused to catch his breath. "If you are not there the Incarnate said he will kill your son . . . Timothy . . . then my mom and dad too."

"Oh, God," Rebecca moaned in horror from the doorway.

"You . . ," Calvin started again. "You're to bring someone named Tasha with you. Both of you are to stand in the middle of the court with the black hoods over your heads. The other hood should be lying around here, somewhere." Calvin blindly turned his head about, as if to look around. "I tried . . . but . . ." With that, he broke and fell into sobbing. "I'm so sorry, Sam."

Samuel picked up the hood that was lying in Calvin's lap. "I got it, buddy," he said. "It's okay, Cal. It's not your fault. Tasha is already here, and we're going to get you to a hospital. Okay, man?"

Calvin's sobbing slowed and he nodded. With his arms freed, Samuel and Tasha lifted him to his feet. Calvin sniffed the air, to clear his nose. "Somebody's perfume smells nice," he said.

"Thank you, Calvin," Tasha said. "I remember you from the bookstore."

"You do?" Calvin asked.

"You're Timothy's biggest fan," she added.

"Well, I'd like to keep that a secret *now*, if you don't mind."

Tasha looked at Samuel and they smiled. "Sure," she said. "It'll be safe with me."

TASHA EXITED THROUGH THE DOORWAY from a hospital's emergency room entrance and walked quickly across the parking lot to her car. She got into the driver's seat, closed the door, and looked over at Samuel. "He's going to be fine, but it's going to take more than a few days." Her eyes went to the rearview mirror then her head turned to the backseat. "Where's Rebecca?" she demanded.

"What do you mean? She was with you."

"She left ahead of me, said she needed some air, and just wanted to go back to the car . . . it was right after the police came in. Oh, my God!" she said. She opened the door and got out of the car. "Rebecca!" she called, looking around the lot. She called several times, then started to walk back toward the emergency room entrance.

Samuel opened his door and jumped out of the car. He rushed up behind Tasha and grabbed her arm. "We don't have time to look for her now," he said calmly.

"She could be in trouble!"

"If we don't leave now innocent people will die."

Tasha looked at him. Slowly the panic in her eye subsided. "Yes," she said, "you're right."

They hurried back to the car, got in, and drove out of the parking lot. Neither of them saw Rebecca, huddled in the shelter of a taxi stop. A cab pulled up and she quickly opened the door and got in. The driver turned around and looked at her. "Where to, ma'am?" he asked.

Less than a mile away from the Thomas Center, Tasha was driving aggressively through the slower moving traffic.

"Be careful," Samuel said. "We can't afford to get stopped."

"Okay, okay," Tasha said. She slowed a little, her face set in concentration. "Tell me one thing, Samuel, is there a heaven?"

Samuel thought a second and shrugged his shoulders. "I don't know . . . I keep coming back." He knew she was looking for more of an answer than he could give her. He smiled. "I guess if there is one, I don't qualify."

"When I read Timothy's book . . . I thought about how incredible it would be to live throughout history from one life to the next." Pausing, she shook her head slowly from side to side. "Now, after meeting you . . . I'm not so sure anymore. I'd always be leaving the ones I love behind . . . never to see them again."

The Spanish Court at the Thomas Center was deserted when Samuel and Tasha arrived. They stood and looked at the dimly lit, colonnaded open court. Samuel looked up at the mezzanine on the second floor. The high ceiling was capped by a full skylight.

"This is one place I'll be sure to remember," he said, his voice subdued. He looked down at the two black hoods he was holding in his hands and held out the one without Calvin's blood stains to Tasha. "Here," he said, giving her a tight smile.

Tasha, fear showing in her eyes, looked at him, nodded, and took the hood. "Why do you think he wanted me here with you?"

"I would guess to find out what you know. Because, he won't be able to get it from me. Incarnates can't read one another. So, don't fight him on it. Tell him everything he wants to know."

She nodded and started to put on the hood, then stopped. "Sam," she said, "if this doesn't . . . end well . . . I hope that you don't remember me in your next life."

"I hope I do," he said. "I'll want to remember that you stood by me." He gave her a smile, moved closer to her side, and draped the black hood over his head.

Tasha took a deep breath and closed her eyes. She put on the hood and reached out, touching Samuel's hand with her fingertips. Samuel took her hand and held it. They waited.

"This is scary," she said after a moment.

Samuel squeezed her hand in gentle reassurance. "It'll be okay," he said. "Try not to be frightened. That's all he's trying to do, right now. Don't give him that." But Samuel wasn't sure about what he was telling her. He really didn't know why Cain wanted her there. For him, as frightened as he was, he knew it didn't matter—at least for himself. He had been born for this very day— the day he would die—one way or another. Tasha was a good soul and, before this night, like Calvin, a happy one. He started to tell himself that he hoped they'd be able to get back to their lives after this was over, but stopped himself. "Who the hell am I kidding," he thought. "It never happens that way, not after the darkness of Cain's presence steps into people's lives." An overwhelming sense of helplessness came to him. Timothy? Surely he would still be alive. Where was he? Was he okay? What could Cain have done? The sudden sound of footsteps came from his left. He turned his head toward the sound.

Six, black robed anhangers stepped out of the darkness of the colonnade. Two of them carried shackles and chains. Samuel felt Tasha's hand squeeze his tightly. Without words, strong hands grabbed them. Tasha screamed in fear, the sound of her voice echoing up against the mezzanine and to the high ceiling above. Forcefully, Samuel and Tasha were separated, pulled apart as they blindly reached out for one another.

REBECCA OPENED THE FRONT DOOR to her parent's home as quietly as she could. She stepped quickly through the living room and down the hall to the master bedroom. Stopping in the doorway, she stood silent, looking at the empty bed—Nathan's bed. A bitter anger came over her.

From one of the walk-in closets, her mother came into the room. Patricia was wearing a bathrobe and drying her hair with a towel. She was halfway to the bed before she noticed her daughter. "Oh!" she said, startled, putting a hand to her heart, "you scared me!" Her eyes searched Rebecca's face. "What's wrong, darling?" she asked in shock. "We've been so worried about you." Her arms out, she started walking towards her daughter.

Holding up her hand, Rebecca stopped her. Rebecca's words came out in a seething tone that her mother had never heard from her before. "Is Nathan here?" she demanded.

Patricia hesitated. "Uh . . . , no," she said.

"Tell me that you didn't know the truth about him."

Her mother's eyes filled with pain. She shook her head. "Honey, what are you talking about?"

"He is not the only one, Mother," Rebecca said. She held her arm out straight and pointed at Patricia. "He lied to us."

"What do you mean?" Patricia said, shaking her head.

"There are *two* incarnates, Mother!" Rebecca screamed. "Another one that is reborn over and over again. They meet in one life after another, slaughtering each other. It's been going on forever—century after century!"

Patricia could only look at her daughter. Reaching out, she took Rebecca into her arms, and held her, rocking her. After a time she leaned back and took her daughter's face in her hands. "No. I didn't know. Oh, baby, I am so sorry." Patricia blinked away from her daughter's stare.

"What is it, Mother?" Rebecca demanded. "There's no time for secrets anymore."

Patricia lowered her head and walked to the bed. She sat, looking down with her hands together in her lap. "There are things . . . things that I haven't told you . . . things that I couldn't tell you. I don't have to be an incarnate to know what you're thinking . . . how could I let such a thing happen to my beautiful daughter?"

Rebecca only looked at her mother warily, tears brimmed in her eyes.

"I'm sorry . . . I thought it was best," Patricia said, she began to wring her hands. "I was torn since the day you were born. Now I know I need to tell you what you don't know." Her voice choked on the last word. She cleared her throat. "Your great-grandfather brought Nathan from Germany after World War Two. He was just an infant and he raised him as one of his own. He always claimed the child was the incarnate of a messiah that would one day rule the world. That is what I was taught to believe from birth. As Nathan got older, it was clear he wasn't a normal child. He knew people—things about people—that he couldn't have known. No one could deceive him. He knew what everyone was thinking before they could even think it themselves. When people listened to him, they believed what he said. He was very smart and always *knew* what to say. He cultivated us with . . . manipulative charm. And he made promises. He promised immortality to those who followed him without question—promised that we would be reincarnated. I was married to your father, who also had fallen under Nathan's spell. He was devoted to him and chose to become an anhanger—to become an elite and unwavering servant of the Incarnate. In doing so, he gave us up. It was as though we had never existed to him. He turned away from his own wife and daughter, in his blind desire to become immortal. Darling, when your father left us, he swore to a life of secrecy. It was very hard for me. I . . . I wasn't strong enough. I became bitter. And in feeling we were so meaningless to him, out of . . . anger . . . spite . . . vengeance . . . I married Nathan. Not out of love, but to become the high priestess of his sect, placing me above all anhangers. Oh, sweetheart," she said. She looked up at Rebecca, stood and walked to her, taking her in her arms. Sobbing, she held and rocked her daughter. "I'm so ashamed I wanted your father beneath me. I never saw him again."

She took Rebecca's hand and led her to the bed. They sat, crying, holding each other.

Patricia had to wipe her eyes before she was able to continue. "But there's more. It didn't take me long to realize my life was an illusion. As high priestess I became nothing more than an icon, and Nathan's . . . concubine. As you grew older, I was horrified to see him becoming attracted to you. I told him that I wouldn't stand for it. He beat me and forbade me to speak of it again. I was so afraid for you . . . I didn't know what to do. I panicked. I took you and ran, desperate to get away . . . anywhere."

Rebecca looked up at her mother. "That was when we went up to that small town in Virginia, staying at that old motel. Wasn't it? You told me you had to go there to see an aunt who was dying."

"Yes, dear, one lie of many, I'm afraid. Of course he found us quickly and we became prisoners. He said if I left again or interfered in any way he'd kill you. I felt I had no other choice than play the role he intended for me. I was horrified when he selected you for the passing. I had no idea what you would do, but I was not allowed to speak other than in support of his will."

"He threatened me, with your life, too. But it wasn't until after I was with Nick," Rebecca said.

"What do you mean?" Patricia asked, her eyes squinting.

"Nathan isn't the father of my baby and . . . I'm having a daughter," Rebecca said. "I never told you. I was so afraid. At the time, I was thinking that Nathan wouldn't have anything to do with me, if he knew I had been with someone, but I became all the more afraid to tell him. So, I didn't." Rebecca began to cry again.

"How could you have kept him from knowing? You couldn't have. He knew and he . . . still took you," Patricia said, her face cringing.

"More times than you know," Rebecca said. Horror came into her eyes and she suddenly stood up, her eyes looking about wildly. "He will know we've spoken. We can't stay here anymore, Mother. We have to leave. We have to leave right now!"

Patricia stood and took Rebecca's shoulders in her hands. "Baby," she said. "There is no place to run. There isn't a place he wouldn't find us. "

Rebecca looked into her mother's eyes. "I don't want us to . . . I *can't* live like this anymore."

"We are not going to," Patricia said. "I'm sorry for all the terrible mistakes I've made. I can't change that." Her eyes narrowed in hard determination. "But if you will trust me, I promise you that I will put an end to it all, and . . . I'll do it tonight."

CHAPTER NINETEEN

TREMBLING WITH TERROR, TASHA STOOD hooded and shackled on a dark green, black sun emblem that was inlaid into the stone floor. Strong hands clasped her by a shoulder and an arm. She was forced to her knees and the black hood was pulled off of her head. Blinking and adjusting to the light, her frightened eyes darted around apprehensively. She was in a strange, large and stark, concrete walled chamber. The flickering of red, amber light dimly lit the room. It was not unlike another century's concept of hell.

An intense heat radiated over her face and body. She looked up; her eyes were drawn to the smoky, fiery glow of a smelter. A large iron ladle was suspended by chains draping down from the ceiling. An anhanger, hooded, masked, and dressed in body armor, attended to the smelter. Several anhangers stood rigidly at attention, while others busied themselves around the chamber. In front of the smelter was a large, iron platform. Four heavy chains at its corners descended from ports cut into the ceiling of the chamber. To her right, three anhangers, their backs to her, huddled about a tall iron armature that resembled a medieval crow's cage.

From behind her, to the left, came the sound of footsteps. An anhanger was leading a man toward her—he too had a black hood over his head. They forced the captive to kneel down to the left of her. The anhanger roughly yanked off the man's hood.

"Oh, my God!" Tasha said. "Timothy!"

Timothy Godwin's face and jaw were bruised and dried blood caked around open cuts and abrasions. Squinting, he looked at Tasha. Their eyes met, in a sharing of fear and hopelessness. Timothy eyes went to the other side of Tasha and his face froze in a pale, sickening stare. Tasha followed his gaze. The anhangers who'd been working around the cage-like apparatus had stepped aside.

Tasha's mouth fell open in shook. She gasped in horror.

Samuel was inside the metal contraption. He was stripped of his clothing and his wrists and ankles were shackled. His face was contorted in agony. The steel bands of the cage that entrapped him were studded every few inches with long, gleaming-sharp, metal spikes pointing inward. Samuel could feel the metal tips all over his body, some cut just into his skin, some prickling, threatening. He desperately contorted himself trying to avoid them.

One of the anhangers reached out and put his hands on a large control wheel that was mounted on the front of the cage. Slowly, he turned the wheel. Its gears clicked, and the torturous monstrosity closed tighter in tiny increments. Samuel grimaced in agony as the spikes began to move deeper into his flesh. He fought to still himself and control the muscle spasms and twitching of his body. The anhanger stepped back. Trickles of blood slowly rolled down Samuel's skin from a dozen places.

Samuel was aware of others on floor near him. Being very careful to avoid impaling himself further, he turned his head and eyes the meager amount the spikes would allow. He could see Tasha and Timothy cowering on the floor looking at him. Tears rolled down Tasha's face. His heart sank. It took all of his strength to muster an encouraging smile. He knew that he wasn't fooling anyone. Shuddering in hopelessness, he turned his eyes away. Suddenly, a wave of anger surged into him. Trying to turn his eyes to one of his captors too carelessly, a spike sank into his cheek. He felt the sting and the warm ooze of blood roll down his face. The dark lenses built into the anhanger's masks made it impossible for him to look into their eyes.

"Can't see your eyes," Samuel snarled in a loud scream. "You want to know what I'm thinking?"

"*I* would," came a voice from a dark tunnel in front of him. A commanding figure, escorted by two anhangers, came sweeping into the room. The man wore a flowing, dark cloak and robe, his face was covered by a gold, skeletal mask. Hanging from a chain around his neck dangled a gold, black sun medallion. All of the anhangers lowered their heads in veneration.

Samuel's chest swelled with the pain and fury of millenniums. Immediately, he knew the man approaching him was the Incarnate. He could see the white, flaming eyes and the ghostly red aura emanating from his body. All questions were gone. This was the *one,* the curse of mankind since the beginning. Samuel was overwhelmed by a vision. A cascading cavalcade of the history of mankind, seen through the eyes of men and women—people of all races and cultures—that were his previous incarnations, poured over him. The images shot through his mind, burning through his soul, in a vast tableau of settings and events: births, deaths, executions, slaughters, and suicides. All the anguish, suffering, and strife that plagued mankind engulfed him . . . endless years of horror washing over him in an instant. Striding in arrogance, the Incarnate stepped onto the iron platform.

Her voice husky with fear and anger, Tasha suddenly called out, "Why hide behind a mask, Nathan? We all know who you are."

The Incarnate came down from the platform, the heels of his boots thudding onto the floor. He stood over Tasha. She looked up at him fearfully as he pulled the hood off of his head and lifted the mask from his face.

"You disgust me," Tasha spit out in anger. "How could you do it? To use your own daughter."

Nathan gave a grunt of mild amusement and, without looking, handed the mask to an anhanger. "Is that all that concerns you right now?" he asked, looking down into her unwavering glare. "Such was the way in the beginning, and I am from the beginning."

Tasha shook her head in revulsion. "You're a sick bastard!"

Anger flashed across Nathan's face, he drew back his arm and slapped her hard across the face. She collapsed to the marble floor.

Timothy scrambled to his feet and tried to lunge at Nathan. He was instantly felled by a blow from the mace of a nearby anhanger.

Nathan, his eyes on Tasha, ignored Timothy. "Insult me again and I will cut out your tongue. Your inability to speak would be of no hindrance to me."

With blood dripping from her lip, Tasha turned her head and glared at Nathan.

Looking intently into her eyes, a smile lifted in the corner of Nathan's mouth. "And I can see you already know that."

While Tasha slowly picked herself up off the floor, Nathan looked over at Timothy. "And you. Try that again and I assure you she will suffer far worse."

Still writhing in pain from the blow of the mace, Timothy looked up at him. "What has she ever done to you, Nathan?" he cried in exasperation.

Nathan raised his head and flared a nostril in contempt. "Nothing of any consequence. You, like her, are innocent and easily manipulated. The innocent have always been used as tools for . . . persuasion."

"Only by those who are evil," Samuel said in a low, steady voice.

Nathan flinched. "You know, I think it's your self-righteousness that I've hated most of all about you." He reached over and put his hand on the wheel latch of the entrapping cage. An evil grin came to his face as he turned the wheel. Four slow clicks of the ratcheting mechanism sounded against the stone walls.

The steel spikes penetrated deeper into Samuel's flesh. A searing wave of pain swept over him. The agony was so intense that, for an instant, he almost blacked out. He let out a gasping scream.

"No!!!" Tasha cried.

Timothy managed to lift himself to his knees. "Why are you doing this?" he pled.

Samuel was trying to overcome the pain. He could feel the points biting into his flesh in so many places, it felt like he'd been thrown into a fire. His body shuddered as he tried to control his breathing enough to speak. "Because . . . of an offering that . . . was rejected. . . . Rejected because of a lack of . . . sincerity."

The words brought an angry, resentful expression to Nathan's face. "Why wasn't it enough that I worked the earth until my hands bled?" he asked. He turned, his eyes burning in fury at his foe. Almost hissing more than speaking, he said, "Why should I have had to give up any of the fruits of my labor to a god or anyone else?"

"Your greed and arrogance blinded you, Cain!" Samuel said. He summoned all of his strength against passing out. "You couldn't see that the fruits of your labor were a gift!"

Nathan's face contorted in bitter rejection of Samuel's words, then recovered with an evil grin. "Well, it's too late now. Isn't it?" Impulsively, he reached out and again turned the wheel. One click. The cage creaked as the spikes dug deeper—there was the unmistakable crack of a bone.

Samuel let out a guttural scream. Shivering, he gave out a scratchy, powerful grunt of effort against passing out. He knew he had to hold on for as long as possible. Whatever was to happen, he needed it to be a part of his memory, right up to the end. Fresh blood began to flow from his wounds, radiating out from the embedded prongs.

Nathan's eyes glowed with the pure evil of transfixing pleasure. "You realize this will be the first time I've killed you twice . . . in one lifetime?" He asked the question with the lilt of a chuckle. With a flip of a hand he signaled the anhangers.

Two of the cloaked figures immediately began to pull on a chain that hung down from the ceiling. There was the ratcheting sound of clinking steel from above. The massive chains that were attached to the iron platform on the floor began to lose their slackness and grow taut. The chains strained as the platform slowly lifted into the air.

Fighting waves of blurred vision, Samuel could see that the top of the platform was a lid that covered a vault. He stared into the darkness of the hole. Instantly, he knew who it was meant for.

"Take a good look, Able," Nathan said. "This will be your resting place for a very long time. The walls are six inches thick," he continued. "Made of pure iron, like the lid hanging above it." He pointed with a long, gloved finger. "With you inside, it will be closed again and sealed air tight by molten iron. I can't help but wonder how you will die in the darkness. Will it be a slow bloody death . . . suffocation . . . dehydration . . . starvation . . . or perhaps infection from the steel spikes that have pierced your body? I hope to never know . . . for at least a few thousand years. You've hindered me long enough."

Nathan turned his back to Samuel and approached Timothy. "As for you," he said. "You shall continue your work as a writer. I will see that you become very wealthy and world renowned with the *Journeymen* series. Although it is currently regarded as fiction, and will continue to be for the most part, you will alter your writing as I see fit. And when the time comes, you *will* proclaim your stories to be based on fact. And I will reveal myself to the world as the one true Incarnate.

"To hell with you!" Timothy yelled.

"Need I remind you of your family?" Nathan said, his voice dripping with detached arrogance. "You don't realize the scope of my vengeance. You will do as I say, or your family will suffer in poverty and pain. Not only them, mind you, but every generation after them . . . forever. I *always* come back."

Timothy's head fell to his chest.

Nathan turned. "Please don't think I'd forget you, my dear Tasha," he said with horrid grin. "I'm still in need of a son."

Tasha's mouth curled in disgust.

"How foolish of you to forget, I know what you're thinking. Then die you will . . . but not until I've had all I want from you."

Tasha spat at his feet, striking the tip of his garment.

Enraged, he grabbed her by the hair and dragged her forward several feet before letting her go. Tasha fell flat to the ground. "I will break your spirit," he said. He'd drawn his fist up into the air when he froze at the sound of the opening of the large iron doors of the ritual chamber. Rebecca stood in the doorway, looking at him. Nathan gave her a questioning look as his fist slowly lowered.

Rebecca glared into his eyes and turned, reaching back into the darkness of the entry tunnel. She led her mother by the hand, into the room.

Patricia was blindfolded. She was dressed in the black, flowing silk gown of an empress; her hands were folded under an ornate sash that ran diagonally across her chest. The two women came forward. The anhangers lowered their heads in reverence as they passed.

Rebecca, her lips trembling and her jaw set in determination, led her mother to stand in front of her husband.

The Incarnate waited with a look of suspicious distaste. They stopped in front of him. He stared into Rebecca's eyes. "What is this? Why are you here?" he demanded. "I've not called for either of you."

Rebecca looked up at him, edging her face yet closer. "I don't know, Father," she said. "Mother asked that I bring her to you and refused to tell me more."

Nathan looked at his wife. "How dare you come to me in this manner! Remove the blindfold," he ordered.

"No!" Patricia spoke slowly, sounding out each word firmly and clearly. " I want you to."

Without hesitation, Nathan reached out and tore the blindfold away. Patricia's eyes blazed with hatred. He shoved her hard just as her hand came out from under the sash and lashed out at him. Nathan's face went slack with shock.

Patricia reached out to grab to Nathan, trying to stop her fall. As she did, her hand clasped onto sun medallion, breaking its chain. The medallion slipped from her fingers as she fell to the ground.

Nathan bent at the waist and staggered back, a hand clutching his side. His eyes were filled with disbelief. Slowly, his face drawn in pain, he straightened. He took the hand from his side and looked at it. It was covered with blood.

Patricia hurriedly got to her feet, brandishing a bloody dagger. Her face twisted with rage, she screamed and lunged at Nathan. In a dark blur, several of the anhangers swept in to block and subdue her.

Furious, Nathan whirled to confront his daughter. He grabbed her by the throat with one hand, holding her tightly. Rebecca was almost lifted into the air, her two hands trying to pry her father's fingers loose. The Incarnate snarled his words at her. "You have betrayed me a second time. I would have found some use for *your* daughter. She will never know you or her *real* father, because your Nick is dead. How stupid of you to think you could keep the truth from me." He threw her to the floor. Immediately, an anhanger pinned her down.

Patricia struggled against the hold of two anhangers as she was brought up to face her husband. Nathan looked at her as though he were looking at a snake. Reaching out, he grabbed the front of her gown, and ripped it open. A wicked smile came to his eyes and he turned to the anhangers. "Have your way with her," he said. He waved a hand to indicate the entire room. "All of you! But," he said, "keep her alive."

"No!!!" Rebecca screamed as they dragged her mother away.

Nathan looked down at his daughter. "Take her too. Be sure she sees everything that is done to her mother," he sneered, "then have the same done to her."

"No!!!" Rebecca screamed again, struggling against the anhanger dragging her away.

"You son of a bitch," Tasha screamed at Nathan, "why can't you just kill them and get it over with?"

"Death is the end of suffering," Nathan said. "Why would I want to give them that?" He raised his eyebrows. "I'm simply punishing the wicked."

"The wicked!" Timothy spat in anger. "How is that girl wicked?"

"Those that defy me are wicked," Nathan answered.

The anhangers had dragged Patricia and Rebecca to the far corner of the chamber. Several anhangers huddled around them like vultures around their prey. The muffled sounds of protest and struggle came from beyond the knot of black cloaks. Nathan looked in their direction, his face content with obscene pleasure, and raised a hand toward them. "Understand this," he intoned in a deep voice, his eyes blazing as he looked around into the eyes of the other captives. "I always return from the dead. No one escapes my wrath. I intend to be feared by every soul on this earth. Man will serve me and do my bidding." He held out his arms, his palms facing upward. "I shall rule over the living and be worshiped as the one, true God!"

Tasha's eyes jerked up and fixed on him as though something had clicked in her brain. Her head snapped toward Samuel.

Drawn to Tasha's sudden movement, Samuel turned his eyes to hers. Instantly, the message came clearly to him in the original Sumerian, "They are watched and heard from above and below, for should they forget whom they serve, judgment shall come swiftly." Samuel's fading eyes brightened. His eyes shot to Nathan then back to Tasha.

Tasha stared hard into his eyes. "Defy him. Challenge his authority!"

Samuel looked at Nathan, "You might want to be a little more careful, Cain."

Nathan walked over to Samuel. "Careful? Who are you to console *me*?"

"Well, I'm just sayin' you never know who you might *piss* off."

"Piss off," Nathan grunted in derision. "Who? Your god? Your god has never opposed me, nor has stopped me from *anything*." Nathan's eye's burned into Samuel's, his whole body trembled in rage. "There is *no one* above me!" Just as the last words left his lips, a strong tremor ran through the chamber, from one side to the other. The blood drained from Nathan's face.

"You have forgotten whom you serve," Samuel said.

An ominous voice echoed through the chamber, "Indeed you have."

Everyone froze, the anhanger's heads turned to Nathan. The Incarnate's face was ashen; his eyes flickered around the chamber in fear. There was movement by the entrance. The anhangers who were standing sentry were backing away in trepidation. Nathan stared in shock. A sleek, sinuous figure was standing at the open entrance of the chamber. Cain's eyes registered immediate recognition and terror.

The room was dead silent. All eyes were irresistibly drawn to and transfixed by the sensuous evil that emanated from the creature. In slow deliberate steps, it gracefully flowed more than moved across the floor. Its fierce glowing eyes, as much as they were terrifying, engendered an irresistible, alluring hedonism.

The anhangers cowered, edging back from the specter before them. Those that held Patricia and Rebecca released their grasp. Rebecca instantly ran to her mother's arms.

The burning-coal, red eyes of the fiend were fixed only on Nathan as it came forward. As it passed the first anhanger, the sentry's body burst into flame. There was a very brief, agonizing scream before he was almost instantly reduced to nothing but wisps of white ash. In quick succession, each of the anhangers, one after another, was consumed in turn as the Devil passed. Freed of their captors, Tasha and Timothy ran to Samuel's side.

From the ceiling above, the chains holding the platform were suddenly red with heat. Quickly turning orange-white they began to stretch and elongate before igniting into flames. With a loud crack, the chains snapped and the heavy lid fell onto the top of the vault with a metallic boom that quaked through the stone floor.

Walking across the covered vault, the Devil stopped in front of Nathan, who for once was muted, helpless, and stood as if unable to move.

"Worshiped as the one true God, Cain?" The Devil asked, its voice hissing with the sound of many voices, echoing from all directions. With one hand the creature reached out and grabbed Nathan, wrapping its long, sinewy fingers around his throat. The Devil gave him a spine-chilling smile that spread almost from ear to ear, its teeth were sharp and yellowed. The sulfurous odor of the creature's breath permeated the chamber. With no apparent effort, it lifted Nathan's limp body, suspending him a foot above the floor. "I am not amused by your arrogance," the Devil said. Slowly it tilted its head from side to side, studying the horrified look in Nathan's eyes. Content, it spoke again. "You were warned, Cain, now you shall suffer for an eternity."

Without hurry, holding his prey at arm's length, the Devil turned and moved across the platform to the smelter. As he neared the ladle, it tipped, pouring white hot, molten iron onto the floor. The Devil thrust its arm forward, forcing Nathan into the burning glow of the stream. Nathan only managed a brief scream of agony before his suffering was cut short by the sizzling, liquid fire. His flesh hissed and sputtered as his body was consumed in a hellish blaze. A white vaporous smoke rose from the last remaining scrap of flesh that remained of the corpse. It swirled slowly, gathering into a thickening cloud, and began to take form. The captives watched as ghostly, demonic eyes and a gruesome, maniacal face formed. The eyes burned in an all consuming hatred. Finally, it let out an angry, shattering screech and instantly dissipated into a mist. The Devil tilted its head back, opening its mouth wide. It inhaled and the mist streamed into the creature's mouth.

The Devil, slowly turning its head, looked into the eyes of each of those in the room in turn—lastly, at Samuel. Then, with an instantaneous flash of radiant flames, it vanished.

Mesmerized by what they'd seen, the captives were slow to react. Rebecca and Patricia cautiously rose to their feet, before running to Timothy and Tasha standing in front of Samuel's trapped, bleeding body. Totally immobilized by the spikes, he could only look down at them with sunken, harrowed eyes. Timothy lurched toward the crank that controlled the deadly spikes.

"No!" Samuel gasped, stopping him. "Don't. It's too late. I'll . . . only die . . . quicker."

"We have to get you to a hospital!" Timothy yelled in anguish.

Samuel scrunched his eyes, indicating "No," then looked at Tasha and Timothy. "It's too . . . late for that. I need you to write down everything . . . that has happened . . . put it in with . . . with the other manuscripts." He paused and took several shallow breaths, summoning what energy he had left. "Calvin will be able to tell you, what you don't know . . . and . . . tell him, I won't forget him. I won't forget any of you."

Tasha, her eyes filled with tears, looked up at him. "What do you want done with the manuscripts?" she asked, struggling to get out the words."

Samuel looked over at Timothy, "You'll know what to do," he said, the wisp of a smile on his fading eyes."

"I don't understand," said Timothy.

"You will."

Rebecca, sobbed, "Is Nathan going to come back?"

"I don't know," Samuel said, his voice weakened now to little more than a whisper. "But if . . . he does . . . I'm sure I will . . . as well. It's . . . time . . ."

"For what," Rebecca asked, her voice almost childlike.

"A new beginning," Tasha said. The life in Samuel's eyes dulled and lost light of life. As the four of them watched, a vaporous, beautiful, angelic entity rose from off Samuel's body. It looked at them reassuringly, then vanished as though it were instantly drawn upward.

Looking up, Tasha's face glowed with reverence. Tears rolled down her face. "Somewhere," she said, "a newborn child is drawing its first breath."

"Oh, my God!" Rebecca suddenly cried out.

They all followed her eyes to the ceiling of the chamber. Flames and thick, black smoke were gushing out of the four ports that the heavy chains descended from. In seconds the smoke thickened to where they could no longer see the ceiling.

"Where the hell are we?" Timothy called out, looking at Rebecca and her mother. "What's above us?"

"The house!" Patricia screamed. "Our home! We've got to get out now!"

Timothy grabbed the wheel of the cage that trapped Samuel's lifeless body. It loosened only a fraction before it locked into place. He grimaced, straining against the wheel. "Help me, I can't get him out!" he yelled.

"We have to go," Patricia said. "If we don't leave now we'll all die!"

"Timothy," Tasha said, putting a hand on his shoulder. "He's not there anymore. You saw that. Now he needs you to tell his story, he'd want us to leave before it's too late."

Timothy stared into Tasha's eyes for only a second before he looked back to Patricia and nodded.

"This way!" Patricia said and, holding Rebecca's hand, ran for the open entry in the stone wall.

Timothy, last behind Tasha, started following when his eyes caught the gold, black sun medallion lying on the floor. He bent and picked it up. Suddenly, he was jarred by a loud boom and a blast of flame from the top of the chamber.

"Timothy!" Tasha screamed from the passageway. "Hurry!"

He ran towards her, stuffing the medallion into his pocket.

They all followed through a tunnel and up a steep, narrow set of stairs to a trap door. When Patricia forced it open, thick smoke quickly engulfed them. "Everyone hold one another's hand, and don't let go!" she screamed. They quickly climbed out through the trap door and into the living room of the house. Patricia led them, running, to the front door. Bursting out of the house, they kept running, not stopping until they collapsed on the lawn of a house across the street. The four of them coughed and gasped for air while they watched the house burn to the ground.

EPILOGUE

TIMOTHY AWAKENED LYING ON THE SOFA in the study of his home. He'd been too exhausted the night before to change clothes or do anything else beyond collapsing. The thick smell of smoke clung to him and brown-red smears of dried blood spotted his clothing. He sat up slowly, groaning from the pain of his wounds and the ache of his muscles. His eyes were clouded with thoughtless exhaustion for a moment before they suddenly came to life. Quickly, he reached into his pants pocket and pulled out the gold sun medallion, he had picked up the night before. With a grimace, he rose and stepped across the room to his desk. As he was sliding out the chair, he stopped short, noticing an unfamiliar pen that was lying on top of the hardcover copy of his book. He picked up the pen. "Meadowbrook Psychiatric Institute" was stamped in gold on the barrel. A look of confusion etched his face. He set the pen down and opened the desk drawer.

"What the . . .?" he said aloud. There were two sun medallions in the drawer, a silver one, he'd never seen before, was lying next to the bronze that he'd found with his father's things. They were both lying on a white envelope. On the outside of the envelope, "Timothy" was written in a handwriting he didn't recognize. He held back for a second before grabbing the envelope and tearing it open. Inside was a letter.

Timothy,

I am sorry that I had frightened you before I remembered who you were. It is so strange to me now, knowing that I could have stood right next to you, without you ever realizing who I was.

At this moment, it is difficult to know what to say, without knowing what will happen or has happened by the time you read this letter. For you to have found it, chances are that I have died again. If so, I can only hope that you have some understanding of who I am and who I have been. Many of the answers you already know. They are written in my journals and the manuscripts I died with when you knew me as your father.

In our brief passing, I can only imagine you think I am delusional. I don't blame you for that. There is no rational reason for you to believe that I could be your father, knowing I was born after you. Although I am physically someone else, I remember you.

In the hope that you believe that I was once your father, I request that you will fulfill the following instructions. Please know that it doesn't matter if it was a previous life, or any life after this, you will always and forever be my son.

Always in my memories and in my heart, your father.

TIMOTHY STOOD IN THE SUN DAPPLED SHADE of a cemetery, a smile of contentment on his face. "Well," he said, "that about does it."

"Yes," Tasha said, "this is the last of the documents." Smiling, she looked at Patricia, Calvin, and Rebecca. "Shall we?"

The five of them, each carrying a hermetically sealed, plastic container, filed into the open door of the new, gleaming white, marble mausoleum. One by one, they laid the containers down on the empty space on a stone bench that lined the walls. The rest of the interior was crowded by all of the relics that had been moved from the St. Augustine mausoleum. Next to the ironwood chest laid Darnell's olive-drab, canvas army bag.

Tasha moved her fingers across the top of the container she'd carried in. "You don't know how much I hate to give these up," she said.

Timothy put a consoling hand on her shoulder.

"I know," Tasha said, "he is going to need them more than me. It's just the researcher in me."

Rebecca looked around the interior, her eyes wide in wonder. "It's really beautiful, Timothy," she said.

"Thanks, but I just followed his instructions. The monument company took care of the rest."

Calvin reached out and took Rebecca's hand. She held his hand in both of hers and gently laid it on her swollen stomach. They looked lovingly into each other's eyes for a moment before he blinked, turned, and smiled shyly at Patricia. "I guess . . . ," he started in a nervous stammer, "there's no . . . sense of coming back. I . . . I mean . . . he's not here. Do you think he'll know that there wasn't anything left of him to bury?"

"He'll know," Timothy answered nodding with certainty. "Or, perhaps it's over and he won't need to. But, if he does . . ." Timothy reached into his pocket and pulled out the three sun medallions and placed them on top of the last container. "Good luck, Dad . . . wherever you are."

They looked at one another, for a second before walking out. Timothy pushed the heavy steel door closed. There was a metallic clank when the latch caught. He stepped back and looked up at the name that was carved into the stone above the door, "Samuel Holden," it read. His eyes moistened, he blinked, and looked at the others with embarrassment. "Well, I guess that's it," he said. "Oh, wait. I almost forgot. One more thing." Leaning over, he picked up the briefcase that was sitting on the stone apron, next to the door of the monument. "It's something for you Calvin." He opened the briefcase and pulled out a paperback copy of *The Journeymen Diaries*. "He . . . , Samuel that is," he said, with a quiet laugh, "wanted me to give this to you."

"Wow. He didn't forget," Calvin said, taking the book. "Ahh . . . could I get you to sign it?"

"I already have," Timothy said, "and someone else did too."

Calvin eagerly opened the book to the title page and read the inscription aloud. "'To Calvin, the best friend I've had, in all the lives I've known. Sam.'" He paused and had to clear his throat before he continued, "'To Calvin, my greatest fan. Timothy Godwin.' Thanks," he said, his eyes filling with tears, "you're right, I am still your biggest fan."

"Great," Timothy said laughing. "Maybe I can get you to buy my second book."

"As soon as it comes out," Calvin said.

"That will be soon, I'll finish it today."

"I can't wait to read it," Calvin said.

Timothy smiled at him. "Actually, Calvin, you're in it.

"Yeah? Really? Cool. What's the title?"

"*The Incarnate*," Timothy said.

ABOUT THE AUTHORS

Kenneth Beason has worked as a theme artist, taking part in the creation of some of the many attractions found at Disney World, Sea World, and Universal Studios. He has also won two national competitions writing screenplays based on his own original stories.

James Cavanagh is a criminologist. He has researched and written on human deviance for many years. Formerly, he worked with the convicted felons who suffered from severe mental illness. Today, he lives in Florida pursuing writing projects.

www.ingramcontent.com/pod-product-compliance
Lightning Source LLC
Chambersburg PA
CBHW070832120626
46556CB00002B/731